WYATT WAS FIRE, THERE WAS NO DOUBT ABOUT IT.

As Annie settled in amid the pillows on her bed, thoughts of the preceding hours she'd spent with him came swirling back to her.

Wyatt was a powerfully compelling, highly sensual man who was trying to figure her out, trying to understand what it was about her that attracted him to her.

Frankly she was surprised he hadn't figured it out yet, because the answer wasn't at all complicated. It was the same reason she was attracted to him. *Chemistry*.

The chemistry the two of them had together was strong enough to rearrange the Rockies. But by all accounts the Rockies were perfectly fine the way they were now and so was she.

She obviously had a decision to make.

From their very first kiss, she'd known they could create fire together. She'd also been aware of the sexual tension that simmered just beneath the surface of every look, every touch, and every word they exchanged.

She knew better than anyone how fleeting and fragile life was. She'd learned to make each moment the best that she could, and then go on without regret.

So when the time came for her to make the decision, and it *would* come, she would simply do as she'd always done. She _____ felt right.

WHAT ARE *LOVESWEPT* ROMANCES?

They are stories of true romance and touching emotion. We believe those two very important ingredients are constants in our highly sensual and very believable stories in the LOVESWEPT line. Our goal is to give you, the reader, stories of consistently high quality that may sometimes make you laugh, sometimes make you cry, but are always fresh and creative and contain many delightful surprises within their pages.

Most romance fans read an enormous number of books. Those they truly love, they keep. Others may be traded with friends and soon forgotten. We hope that each LOVESWEPT romance will be a treasure—a "keeper." We will always try to publish

LOVE STORIES YOU'LL NEVER FORGET
BY AUTHORS YOU'LL ALWAYS REMEMBER

The Editors

THE DAMARON MARK: THE MAGIC MAN

FAYRENE PRESTON

BANTAM BOOKS
NEW YORK · TORONTO · LONDON · SYDNEY · AUCKLAND

THE DAMARON MARK: THE MAGIC MAN

A Bantam Book / March 1998

ISBN 0-553-44534-0

Published simultaneously in the United States and Canada

*Bantam Books are published by Bantam Books, a division of Bantam Dou-
bleday Dell Publishing Group, Inc. Its trademark, consisting of the words
"Bantam Books" and the portrayal of a rooster, is Registered in U.S.
Patent and Trademark Office and in other countries. Marca Registrada.
Bantam Books, 1540 Broadway, New York, New York 10036.*

PRINTED IN THE UNITED STATES OF AMERICA

OPM   10 9 8 7 6 5 4 3 2 1

To Mona Sizer
for introducing me to the magic of
John Donne

ONE

Mist hovered over the northwestern glacier lake and swirled across the path along which Wyatt Damaron walked. Above him, silver-gray clouds drifted across the sky, occasionally breaking apart to show an almost full moon, mystical and majestic, its light eerie as it reflected off the mist and filtered through the woods that lay just beyond the path.

To his right, the gentle lapping of water indicated the lake washing against the shore, but the mist distorted the sound and hid the lake, making it hard for him to tell exactly how far away it was. To his left, the faint, distant sound of music came to him, faded away, then floated back—unrecognizable music, delicate, melodic, and haunting.

The night had an otherworldly feel about it, as if spirits might be walking abroad, he reflected, then smiled inwardly at the thought. He probably should have waited until morning to investigate his surroundings, but the trip had left him too restless to sleep and he'd decided to strike out from the cabin to explore. He hadn't gone too far, though, before he'd realized he needed to proceed with caution.

The mist swirled in ghostly currents, opening up the path before him for several yards, then closing it again without warning. It was disorienting, and he had to remain alert and pay attention to where he stepped.

Leaves rustled around him. A sudden breeze shivered across the lake and into the mist, and the wraith-like vapor responded, gathering and building, until one ethereal layer was stacked atop another.

A night bird called drowsily. Another, perhaps its mate, answered. Pebbles rattled faintly. Wyatt stopped. No breeze or fog could move a pebble. Something or someone was coming toward him. His muscles tightened.

On the path in front of him a shape appeared. He held his breath. Then out of the silvery mist a woman materialized. Her long skirts, one dark and hitched so that he could see the bottom skirt of lace, disappeared into the swirling vapor, making it appear as if she were floating. Her blond hair fell straight and shimmering over her bare shoulders. A coronet of some sort rested atop her head, and its long ribbons fluttered in the soft breeze.

His first impression was that she had been formed from the mist of another time, but he knew that couldn't be true. He knew for a fact that he was in the Pacific Northwest in the latter days of the twentieth century.

Her eyes widened as she saw him, and she hesitated, the mist curling and curving around her, threatening to take her back.

His first thought became huskily spoken words. "Who are you?"

She half turned away from him as if ready to flee.

Instinctively his hand shot out toward her. "Wait. Don't leave. I won't hurt you."

Slowly she turned back as if something he'd said or done had interested her, and the mist mimicked her movement, swirling in the same direction as she, then curling upward to partially conceal her. "No? You wouldn't offer offense to a lady out and about alone on such a dark night, Sir?"

Sir? Offense? Was she speaking with an accent? English perhaps? Canadian? He couldn't be sure. "Offense? Uh, no—I won't hurt you." Anxious to reassure her, he hurried on. "I'm staying at a cabin not too far from here. It's Scott Westerman's cabin. Maybe you know him?"

She gazed at him for a moment, and he had the strangest feeling she was looking deep into him, weighing his soul, reading the secrets that he carried. Suddenly she nodded and Wyatt received the impression that she'd come to a decision, rather than had answered his question.

She cocked her head to one side, sending blond hair and satin ribbons tumbling over her shoulder and down over one breast. "You're out and about quite late, m'lord. Are you lost?"

M'lord? "Lost?" Perplexed, he shook his head, wondering if he was hearing her correctly.

"Lost," she repeated, and began to glide toward him. " 'Tis easy enough to happen. A stranger finds himself stepped off the edge and into the lake and perhaps meets a kelpie or a water sprite."

"Who *are* you?" he asked, thoroughly confused now.

She held out her skirts and curtsied. "I'm the Lady Anne of the Court of King Henry, m'lord."

It didn't make sense, he thought. No sense whatsoever.

The coronet on her head was made of flowers, he noted as the floral scent reached out to tease his senses. His gaze dropped to her breasts, pushed enticingly high by the tight-fitting dress that stopped directly beneath them, and he saw now that the low-cut sheer blouse that came up to partially cover her breasts was more like a chemise with long, full sleeves. What kind of clothing was that to wear for a walk in the mist so close to midnight? For that matter, what was she doing all alone in such an isolated place?

"And your name, m'lord?" she asked.

"Name? I'm Wyatt Damaron."

"Sir Wyatt of Damaron? I am honored indeed. Yours is a noble name." She curtsied again, all grace and femininity.

"Er, yes. I suppose so." He couldn't tell what color her eyes were, but he thought he caught a hint of a twinkle in them. Suddenly he realized what she'd said.

"No—that is, Wyatt is my first name. Damaron is my last."

"You are saying you are *not* a nobleman?" She cocked her head to the other side and slowly circled him, studying him as if she found him an oddity.

He returned the sentiment, he thought wryly. Odd didn't begin to cover the things she was saying. And her dress—it was velvet, its front and oversleeves embroidered with gold thread and studded with jewels that glittered in the moonlight. His own sense of humor awakened as he answered her. "I'm not sure."

"You are most handsome of countenance, m'lord," she said, returning to stand in front of him.

"Thank you. And you are incredibly beautiful."

His compliment didn't seem to affect her one way or the other.

"Are you perchance one of the king's gamekeepers?" she asked.

He was dreaming. What other explanation could there be? A beautiful woman had appeared out of the mist and looked and talked as if she were from another time. He *had* to be dreaming—and he wasn't ready to wake up. "Sure," he said. "Why not? I'm a gamekeeper."

She nodded, her expression serious, as if she now understood. He wished he could say the same.

" 'Twas the silver mark in your hair that led me to think you of noble birth."

"Oh, I assure you I *am* noble." As long as it was a dream, he figured he could be anything he wanted, he could *do* anything he wanted.

"But you said . . . Ah, never mind. I see you were jesting with me. So, Sir Wyatt of Damaron, have you traveled far, perhaps from one of the eastern kingdoms?"

"Whatever you say." He reached for her, intending to draw her into his arms, but she effortlessly eluded him, dancing away, light as a fairy. "Wait. Stay."

"Remember your promise," she said, her tone half reproach, half laughter. "You promised not to harm me."

"I won't. I wasn't." He threw out his hands toward her but caught himself and just as quickly pulled them back. "I only wanted to touch you."

"Why?"

"To see if you were real."

"Oh, yes, m'lord—very real, at least for this night."

"This night?"

Slowly she smiled. "Come with me. Warm thyself by our fire."

He blew out a long breath. Why fight it? "Sure, why not?"

He followed her through the woods, and always she stayed just out of his reach. Amidst the trees, the mist was thicker than it had been along the path, and he almost lost her more than once. Was she real or not? She had said she was, at least for this night. No way did that make sense.

Was it really possible that somewhere in the mist he'd crossed into a different time without being aware of it? Or maybe he'd fallen asleep and he was now in the middle of a dream? No, neither one of those things could be possible.

Voices. Laughter. Suddenly he realized he was hearing other things than just the haunting music that had been floating toward him as he walked. And it was all growing louder and louder as he went along.

"Hey," he yelled to her. "Wait up."

With a laugh that sounded like crystal bells, she threw a glance at him over her shoulder. "You have forgotten my name already, Sir Wyatt. My name is Lady Anne."

He hadn't forgotten, but calling her by the name she had given him was giving credence to the fantasy in which they seemed to be. He wanted this situation to be reality. He *needed* her to be real.

Where was she?

He muttered a curse beneath his breath. "Then, Lady Anne, *wait up.*"

Again the crystal bells pealed as her laughter floated back to him. "You've not much farther to go, Sir. Your ears can lead you now. *Oh—*"

"What? What is it?" Finally he caught up to her, but only because she was at last standing still.

"My ribbons—" She frowned with displeasure. Her slender arms were raised as she worked to free the ribbons and hair, lifting her breasts even higher above her blouse and further revealing their firm, round shape.

The ribbon streamers from the circlet of flowers on her head had caught on a low tree branch. "Your hair's tangled too," he murmured, looking down at her. A shaft of bright moonlight split through the clouds and the tree branches to shine down on her face. Her eyes, he saw for the first time, were a clear blue, and her skin looked like ivory.

"Oh, *fie*," she said in frustration.

He didn't care how out-of-time she spoke, he reflected ruefully, she *had* to be a real flesh and blood woman. She had fire zinging through his veins and hardening his loins.

"Be still," he whispered thickly, moving aside her fingers. "You're making it worse." Taking over the rescue effort, he bent his head close to hers and began to disentangle the silk of her hair and the satin of her ribbons. The scent of flowers and woman filled his nostrils. The face of an enchantress looked up at him.

He could barely concentrate on what he was doing. She, whoever she was, had to be the definition of temptation.

"You're most kind to come to my aid, Sir Wyatt of Damaron," she said softly.

"Be still," he said again, his voice rough as he successfully freed two lengths of ribbon. He lowered his arms, thinking to take a deep breath and regain control of his senses. But as he did, his fingertips brushed the tip of one breast and electricity scored through him. She went very still, barely breathing.

Fire skimmed along his veins and pooled in his belly. His mind ignited with thoughts of lowering her through the mist to the forest floor, stripping the velvet, the lace, and the sheer white fabric from her body and taking her.

His hands shook. With great deliberation he finally

freed more of the ribbons and a length of hair, and this time when his fingers brushed the silky skin of her breast, he allowed them to linger on the softness and warmth.

"I trust, kind Sir," she said softly, her breath and words uneven, "that a man of your breeding and position would not take advantage of a lady who cannot defend herself."

"I said I wouldn't hurt you," he said gruffly, freeing the last of the ribbons and hair. "I never said I wouldn't take advantage of you." He trailed his fingers over the tops of her breasts, then grasped her upper arms and drew her to him. "But I won't. Say the word and I'll stop."

She quivered, but she didn't resist, and when he slowly lowered his mouth, she raised her face as if anticipating his lips on hers. He accepted the invitation. In fact, at this point he wasn't sure he could stop even if she did ask. Thankfully, though, she didn't, and his mouth pressed down on hers and began coaxing her lips apart. His tongue slid into her mouth and over hers, and pleasure and heat jolted through him at the contact. He increased the pressure of his kiss, then thrust his tongue deeper. She made a soft sound of gratification, and a thrill of possession surged through him.

What difference did it make that none of this made sense? She was a woman, warm and willing in his arms, and he wanted her more and more with each beat of his heart. This woman had the face of an angel and a body of fire. She had the power to mystify and inflame him.

On this night that was mystical and mysterious, dark

and shining, strange and wonderful, she had walked out of the mist and into his life, and he didn't think he was going to let her go anytime soon.

She yielded to his kisses and softened against him. With a groan, he gathered her tighter, deepening the kiss, drinking up her taste, intensifying the pleasure. Moments passed, moments filled with fiery kisses and heated touches. Moments filled with intimate caresses and daring thoughts.

Her hands gripped his shoulders, restlessly glided around his rib cage, flattened against his chest . . . and then pushed. "No."

Immediately he released her.

Ribbons and hair brushed against his face as she turned around and disappeared into the mist. He tried to stop her, but his hands closed around air. Without a thought, he went after her.

Suddenly he was in a clearing, and music, laughter, and light exploded around him. Men and women dressed in clothing from another time and place laughed and danced around a bonfire that shot flames into the night sky. Blinking, he paused and attempted to get his bearings. Pipes, stringed instruments, and a hand drum filled the air with the lyrical, now lighthearted music he'd been hearing. Celtic music, he at last realized.

But where was *she*? Wyatt scanned the area in vain for the woman who appeared out of the mist and with equal ease vanished back into it.

"Ho! What's this? A stranger comes among us?" A man wearing a poet's shirt, leather pants, and vest moved into Wyatt's field of vision. He bowed with a sweep of full sleeve. "Sir?"

"I'm Wyatt Damaron."

"Welcome, Sir Wyatt of Damaron. We are honored to have thee among us."

"Thank you, uh, do you know where I can find—?"

The man whirled away and strode into the shadows.

"Come, join the merriment, Sir," a young woman called as she skipped past him. Her dress was simple, high-necked and long-sleeved, but beneath a full, flaring skirt, she wore slippers tied with scarlet ribbons.

"Ale, m'lord?" another man asked before his arm was caught and he was pulled away to join a laughing group.

"Excuse me." Wyatt held out his hand to stop the next person who came near, a lovely young woman wearing a long skirt and a plain white blouse with a gathered neckline and a black waistband that laced up the front. He kept his hand lightly on her arm to ensure she wouldn't escape him before he got his answer. "Do you know where I can find a Lady Anne?" he asked. He felt foolish asking for a Lady Anne, but it was the only name he had for the extraordinary creature who had fired his imagination and inflamed his body.

"She is near, m'lord, of that I am sure," she said pleasantly, then glanced down at his hand on her arm and gasped. "Oooh! What magic is *this*?" Tentatively she touched his watch. "Your wrist shines as brightly as the moon."

"It's a watch." Now he really did feel stupid. But at least he still *knew* he was wearing a watch, which gave him hope. Perhaps he hadn't entirely lost his mind, not yet at any rate.

"A watch, m'lord? Is this something wondrous and new from Far Cathay? Are the eastern trade routes open this time of year?"

Why fight it? he thought. "Yes, yes, they are."

"And your odd dress, m'lord?" She tentatively touched his white cashmere sweater. "Did that too come from Far Cathay?"

"Actually, it came from a small marketplace called Emporio Armani." He shook his head at himself. "I need to find Lady Anne. Please, can you tell me where she is?"

"You asked for me, m'lord?"

She materialized beside him so fast, he almost jumped out of his skin. "Where have you been?" he asked, the harshness in his voice surprising him, though it didn't seem to affect her.

Her face was flushed, her eyes were sparkling. "Here." The sweep of her arm indicated the clearing. "How may I help you? Do you require food or drink?"

"I require *you*."

Her eyes widened, then dark lashes swept down to veil her thoughts, and with perfect composure, she turned to gesture to a pretty redheaded woman wearing a white blouse tied with a drawstring in the center of the low-cut neckline.

The young woman gave a flirtatious toss of her head and sashayed over, a platter of cheese and meat on her hip. Reaching them, she held out the platter and gazed seductively up at Wyatt through a thicket of lashes. "Do you see anything that pleases you, m'lord?"

The Lady Anne gave the other woman a quelling look, Wyatt noted, and when she spoke to him, her voice carried an edge to it. "Would you care for food, m'lord?"

"No, I wouldn't care," he said, his words uttered through gritted teeth, but his tone eased to politeness when he glanced at the redhead. "Thank you, but no thank you." She shrugged and sashayed back to the group she'd been with, and he turned to the woman who was obviously trying to drive him crazy. "Who are these people?"

"Gentle souls who mean you no harm," she said with soft reassurance. "Be not afraid."

Frustration surged but was quickly controlled. "I'm confused, but I'm not afraid. There's a difference."

"As you wish."

He lifted his hand and traced it down the side of her face. "Are you also a gentle soul who means me no harm?"

"Harm you, Sir?" she asked, seemingly startled by the thought. She stepped backward until his hand dropped away from her. "It is not in my nature to harm anyone."

"It may not be in your nature," he said softly, "but you definitely have the ability to do serious harm to a man's heart."

She gazed up at him and in that moment he would have given just about anything to know what she was thinking. She was holding her breath again, leaning slightly toward him, poised on her toes to take flight, yet seemingly unable to move. Behind her, fiery sparks rose and drifted on the air currents. A couple danced by and then were gone. Somewhere there was a shout of laughter. From somewhere else came the delighted squeal of a young girl. Not too far away a young man juggled fruit and yet another juggled torches of fire.

Then she blinked and caught her breath.

And he couldn't take his eyes off the woman who called herself Lady Anne. "All you'd have to do would be to look at a man, perhaps kiss him like you just kissed me in the woods—then tell him he would never have you. I guarantee his heart would never be the same."

Something flickered in her eyes. "But not *your* heart, m'lord."

"Why would you think I'm an exception?"

"Because of who you are."

"And who am I?"

"As you said, not a gamekeeper." She studied him, then reached out and touched the silver streak that ran from his forehead straight back through his hair. "Quite obviously, you are a sorcerer, capable of wondrous magic."

He chuckled huskily. "Well, that's certainly a new one."

"And you are a traveler from one of the eastern kingdoms who must be very weary from your journey." She swept a tankard off a passing tray and handed it to him. "This is mead, m'lord. A drink of honey and spices that in great amounts may sweep your legs from under you and lay quiet your mind. Perhaps in a small amount it will improve your humor and relieve your weariness."

"Perhaps," he said, taking a sip of the sweet wine, but keeping his gaze on her. "And if not, another kiss from my lady's lips will for sure."

"M'lord, another kiss would be most improper."

"Really? And why is that? Is it the rule of your kingdom that one kiss is fine, but two kisses are improper? The lads of the kingdom must be dim indeed if they buy that one. Kiss me, my Lady Anne, and I can promise you the kiss will be most improper indeed."

She tensed ever so slightly, as if she were contemplating taking flight once more. His fingers met as he folded them around her wrist. "Don't leave me again."

She drew in a breath and stared up at him, her eyes wide, her mouth partially open as if she wanted to say something.

"*Hey, Annie!* I was looking for you a while ago and someone said you went for a walk." A gangly teenage boy around seventeen jogged up to her. He was wearing blue jeans, a Seattle Seahawks T-shirt, and a wide smile on his freckled face. "How come you didn't tell me? I would have gone with you and protected you from all the tigers and bears and—"

"Annie?" Wyatt said softly, and the otherworldly mood around them began to dissipate. Suddenly he could see the light touch of mascara on her lashes, the hint of blush and lipstick on her lips and cheeks, the twentieth-century settings holding the jewels on her gown. *Thank God.* She was very beautiful, and she was very real. "Annie," he said again.

Tensed, she still managed to smile. "Hi, Harley. Thanks just the same, but I wasn't gone that long and there were no tigers or bears out tonight. Only . . ." She glanced at Wyatt.

"Hey, did you hear about Zelda?" Harley asked, plainly unaware of what he'd just interrupted. "Word is she's hooked up with a faire in Arkansas." He laughed. "Man, they don't know what they're in for."

"Sorry," Annie said to Wyatt. "Harley sometimes forgets his manners and talks out of turn, not to mention blurting out things a stranger to our area wouldn't care anything about."

Totally unaffected by Annie's gentle reproach, Harley eagerly spun toward Wyatt. "Oh, well. Zelda's lived here for about a year and was a part of this year's faire. But Annie discovered Zelda was selling herbs with labels that made bogus claims and went to the faire director with the info." Harley hooted with delight. "The guy fired Zelda on the spot and she exploded, throwing threats right and left, but mainly at Annie. It was a real blast. Zelda was the big news during the faire."

Annie smiled dryly at Wyatt. "Which should show you just how boring we can be around here. Harley, try to pay attention to me for just a minute, because I want you to meet someone. This is Mr. Wyatt Damaron. Wyatt, this is Harley Jones, a good friend of mine."

Harley gave Wyatt a guileless, thoroughly unimpressed smile and held out his hand. "Nice to meet you, Mr. Damaron."

In the face of such unabashed friendliness, Wyatt couldn't help but smile back. Besides, when he replayed this little scene in his mind, he had the feeling he was going to owe Harley a large debt of gratitude. "Call me Wyatt, Harley." He shook the youth's hand. "Nice T-shirt, but aren't you out of uniform?"

With a laugh Harley glanced down at his T-shirt. "Every year Annie and the others nag me about wearing Ren Faire duds, but hey, there's just no way." He shuddered for effect. "You'll never catch me wearing spandex and a codpiece. It just wouldn't be cool."

"Not cool, huh? So then why are you hanging out here?" Annie's tone carried a teasing affection that Wyatt found very appealing.

"Hey!" Harley looked wounded. "It's the last night of the faire, and I wanted to say good-bye to my friends." He adjusted his T-shirt, his expression playfully affronted. "Do you mind?"

She laughed. "Then quit hanging around me and go say good-bye. They'll be leaving in the morning."

"I'm going. I'm going. See you tomorrow after school."

She nodded. "See you."

"*Annie?*" Wyatt cocked one eyebrow.

She shrugged, relaxed again. "Some people call me Annie."

"Some?"

She grinned. "Quite a few actually."

"Lady Anne" fit the woman who had materialized out of the mist before him. Annie fit the woman standing in front of him now with twinkling blue eyes and a mischievous grin on her soft lips. And both fascinated the hell out of him. "And so this"—he gestured around the clearing—"is a Renaissance Faire?"

"Actually this is a party for the end of the faire here. Tomorrow most of these people will pack up and head off for another part of the country."

"Most?"

"A few here tonight are local."

He looked around him, appraising the frolicking couples. "So if the faire is officially over why did they stay in character for the party?"

"It's natural for them to do that when they're in costume. And the fact that you were a stranger kicked them into gear."

He nodded. "A stranger from one of the eastern kingdoms, right?"

She grinned. "I would say New York would qualify as an eastern kingdom, wouldn't you?"

"Not before tonight I wouldn't have."

She smiled. "At any rate you are most welcome here, Wyatt Damaron. Enjoy the rest of your evening."

"Wait. You explained why the faire people played along, but what about you? Are you with the faire?"

"Not really. While they're here, I run a stand that sells local crafts, and I've gone with them on to their next stop once or twice, but I'm by no means on the circuit. I'm just a friend who enjoys the fun."

"The fun? Is that the reason for the act when we first met?"

She thought for a moment, then shrugged. "The answer's the same as before. I was in costume, and it

seemed natural." She paused. "Plus, Scott had told me
you were coming, so I knew who you were."

"You know Scott?"

"Sure. Everyone knows him."

He wasn't surprised, Wyatt thought wryly. In all
these years he'd never known Scott to meet a stranger.
And when it came to a beautiful woman, Scott went into
overdrive. No woman he'd ever known could resist his
easy charm. The idea that Annie was Scott's friend
didn't make him at all happy and the fact that it didn't
brought Wyatt up short. Since when had he ever been
jealous of Scott?

She started off again, but then stopped and looked
back at him. "By the way, did you find the note I left on
the front table at Scott's, saying he'd be delayed?"

"*You* left the note?"

She nodded. "Scott called a couple of days ago and
asked me to."

"Did he happen to say how long he was going to be
delayed?"

"No, but then with Scott we never know. He comes
and goes on his own schedule." She lifted her hand.
"Good-bye."

This time he fought against the urge to call her back
and was rewarded and surprised when she returned to
him on her own. She reached up to touch the silver
streak in his hair. "You want to know something, Wyatt
Damaron?"

The perfume of the flowers in her hair and the scent
of her skin went straight to his loins, hardening, inflam-
ing. "I absolutely do," he said huskily.

"If I were the kind of woman who fell in love, I could fall in love with you very easily." She graced him with a beautiful smile. "Oh, and don't worry. You won't have any problem finding your way back to the cabin. Just follow the path you were on and you won't get lost."

He already felt lost, he reflected, watching her disappear into the crowd. He also felt utterly astonished and bewildered.

Had he heard her correctly? He couldn't have.

He had.

He was shaking, he realized. Briefly he thought about following her, but decided against it. She'd said she wasn't one of the Ren Faire people, which meant she must be local. If he chose, he'd be able to find her again.

If he chose. . . .

He was tired. He'd conducted a full day of business in New York, then flown hours to get here, only to be ensnared by a woman whose kiss and beauty had left him shaken and whose directness had left him flustered.

The best thing for him to do was to go back to the cabin and get some rest. Hopefully Scott would show up soon. He had a *lot* of questions for him.

Annie closed the door of her house behind her and gave a sigh of relief. She loved being with her Ren Faire friends, but after days spent with them, she always found herself longing for the peaceful sanctuary of her home.

She threw a glance at the hall table, then inwardly smiled, reassured by the sight of her family photographs displayed in perfect order. As she made her way into the kitchen, switching on lights as she went, she pulled the flower wreath from her hair and tossed it onto the sofa. She wasn't hungry, but a cup of tea would be nice.

She set about making it from her own special blend of different teas, which she kept in a pottery container on the counter. Minutes later, she sat down at her kitchen table and sipped contentedly.

In retrospect she had done smarter things in her life than bait and tease Wyatt Damaron, but when she'd met him on the path, it hadn't occurred to her to be on guard. Scott had told her all about the man. They were old friends and for some time they had been trying to get together for a fishing trip. Finally they'd managed and now Wyatt was here. Innocent enough. But Scott had also informed her that Wyatt was a member of the famous Damaron family. But even if he hadn't told her, the silver streak in Wyatt's hair would have. That streak meant great power and wealth. Still, because she knew Wyatt to be a friend of Scott's, she'd initially approached him with the same sense of fun and ease she'd always had with Scott.

It hadn't been too long before she'd realized that Wyatt Damaron was a different type of man than she was used to, and that under normal circumstances, he would require a whole different approach. But for some reason, she'd continued to string him along. Foolish maybe, but fun, and knowing he was only a visitor to their area helped. Soon he would be gone and it would be as if he'd never even been there.

As it happened, however, her sense of fun hadn't helped her when her hair had caught in the branches. Fire had burst to life inside her when he'd kissed her, along with a pleasure so vivid and bright, it had proven almost impossible for her to pull away.

Wyatt Damaron was most definitely a man unlike any other.

He was tall and well built, with a strong jaw and firm, full lips, and when she'd put her hands on him, she'd felt the shift of taut muscle beneath his cashmere sweater.

But it had been his eyes that had really gotten to her—hooded, world-weary eyes ringed with smudges that made them seem even darker than they already were. Danger glinted in those eyes and passion sparked.

Unfortunately by the time she'd noticed the danger and the passion, her course had been set, and she'd continued with her little charade. Why not? No harm had been done.

But somehow during their time together, the realization had come to her. Even after she'd been ready to say good-bye to him, she hadn't been able to stop herself from going back and telling him the truth. If she were prone to falling in love, she could easily fall in love with him. But then, what woman wouldn't?

She took a last drink of tea, set the cup in the sink, and headed for her bedroom. For the first time, she realized she was tired. Her encounter with Wyatt

Damaron had left her keyed up and tense. So much so, she was truly surprised at herself.

After all, she reminded herself, he was only a man. No matter how much money he had, or how intriguing his eyes were, or how well he could kiss, he was only a man. And she probably wouldn't even see him again.

Humming under her breath, she entered her bedroom and switched on the light. And froze.

On the table by the window sat a vase of freshly cut bloodred roses. They hadn't been there when she'd left that morning.

Someone had been in her home.

TWO

Wyatt drew in a breath of the crisp, cool morning air. From the porch of the cabin, he could see the sun already halfway up. It was a promise of a warm, clear day ahead. Scott had raved about the area for years, and he was looking forward to seeing it without the cloaking mist. Now all he needed was for Scott to get back and their vacation could start. He turned around and went back into the cabin for his fourth cup of coffee.

He'd been up for hours conducting business. He'd had to use his cell phone, since Scott had always refused to have a line installed at the cabin. But a couple of hours ago his phone had conked out on him. He'd assumed the battery was dead, but after two hours of trying to get it to hold a charge, he'd had to face the fact that the phone had gone bad.

He planned to go into town to see if he could buy another and to look around for a place to eat while he was there. He also needed to look for a few other things. Hell, he might as well admit it. He would be looking for one particular person.

Annie. Lady Anne.

Her image floated into his mind, and he hardened with desire. What was it about her? He'd spent a restless night unable to get her out of his mind or his dreams.

He wanted to see her in the light of day without the mystery of moonlight and the veil of mist. He wanted to see what she'd be wearing and hear how she would speak. He wanted to see if she'd still smell of flowers and her own personal scent that he'd found so enticing.

He just flat out wanted to see her.

Unfortunately he didn't have a clue where to start looking.

The breeze blew through the windows and across the wind chimes, filling the air with clear, soothing, bell-like tones. Annie dusted the ruby-red vase that she'd just uncrated, the latest work from Archie Shea, a glassblower who exhibited and sold his works in her shop. It went up on the shelf next to the emerald-and-sapphire-colored vases he'd brought her last week. When it came to glass, Archie was one of the best. His work always sold very well.

After disposing of the crating, Annie sat down behind the counter and returned to the account books she'd been working on that morning. Her shop, among other things, was a place for local artisans to show their crafts, and it did very well for everyone concerned. Already there'd been a trickle of tourists through the shop along with one or two of her friends.

A constantly steaming teapot, a large selection of herbal teas, and several comfortable chairs by the fireplace ensured that her shop often became a gathering place for friends and acquaintances. She loved this life she'd created for herself—a life of simplicity, filled with happiness and free of stress. For the most part it was exactly as she wanted it.

Unfortunately, today she had a slight headache. She'd also had a dizzy spell earlier. She'd been having both headaches and dizzy spells for several weeks now. Some were worse than others, but she hadn't allowed them to slow her down. As soon as she had a chance, though, she was going to make an appointment to have her eyes checked. Too much book work, most likely, and no doubt she needed a pair of reading glasses.

She sat back and rubbed an aching spot between her eyebrows. She wished she didn't feel so wary and nervy. But the memory of the roses she'd found in her home the night before was casting a shadow over what would normally be a great day.

Distressingly, the roses weren't the first incident at her home. Over the last month there had been a series of mysterious hang-ups. At first she'd dismissed them as wrong numbers, but the silences that had greeted her on the phone had turned ominous and the hang-ups had become too numerous to ignore. Unfortunately their small town had no caller ID.

Then things had started disappearing—favorite hair clips, a special pair of earrings, an antique compact, a bracelet. She'd initially thought she'd misplaced the items, but the day had come when she'd had to admit the possibility that someone had been in her home and taken them.

Troubled and unable to fathom a reason why someone would want her things, she'd had her locks changed. After that nothing else had turned up missing. But just as she was breathing a sigh of relief, she began to notice the family photographs in the front hallway were out of place.

Nothing too obvious at first. Two pictures switched, each in the other's position. It was something she might have absently done when she was dusting, though it was something she'd never done before. The pictures were important to her, particularly those of her dad, and she liked them arranged in a certain way. She'd returned the pictures to their original places, but two days later *all* of them had been rearranged. She'd had her locks changed again, and the roses had been her reward.

She'd considered and dismissed the idea of going to the county sheriff with her worries because she already knew what would happen. He'd ask a few questions, then file her complaint away and forget about it. In his last term as sheriff, he had demonstrated plenty of times before that he couldn't care less about her and her artist friends whom he called hippies.

And truthfully none of the things that had happened were harmful to her. She'd received no threats. No, it was almost like someone was trying to gaslight her, make her question her mental stability. But why? Did they want to make her reach out for help to someone? Again why? And who?

The opening of her front door brought her out of her reverie. Her best friend, Deb Jenkins, who owned a dress shop across the street, swept into the store, her green eyes glowing with excitement.

"I can't be gone from the shop long at all," she said, her words coming out in a rush, "but I had to come over and find out about the hunk you were with last night." She glanced at her watch. "You've got thirty seconds to tell me everything. *Go.*"

"I wasn't *with* him," Annie replied calmly. "I encountered him when I went for a walk. We talked, and I brought him back to the bonfire." As close as she was to Deb, she found herself wanting to keep the kiss she'd shared with Wyatt to herself.

"Uh-huh. *And?*"

"And that's it. He's a friend of Scott's. They've planned a little fishing vacation together, and I probably won't see him again."

"Well, drat!"

Annie grinned at her friend's crestfallen expression. "Sorry."

"Yeah, okay. Well, I gotta go." Deb snapped her fingers. "Oh, I almost forgot. I've got some gossip. Did you hear about Zelda landing a job with a faire somewhere in the South? Arkansas, I think."

"Harley told me last night." She shook her head. "Surely they won't let her sell her herbs without checking her credentials."

"Well, look what happened here. If you hadn't

dropped a word in the ear of the Ren Faire director, he would have taken her word for it that she had a license."

"But all faire directors can't be as casual about things like that as he was."

"Who knows?" she said. "She sure was furious with you, but she's gone now. That little house she's been renting on the edge of town is all closed up, and there's already a For Rent sign out in front of it. See you later."

Just as Deb reached the door, a sandy-haired man walked in.

"Hi, Dennis," Deb said. "Bye, Dennis."

"Bye, Deb," he called after her.

Annie studied the man as he approached her. He was Dennis Patterson, a teacher who taught shop and history at the local high school. She'd always thought he was good-looking in a rumpled, preppie sort of way, but she wasn't particularly glad to see him. "What are you doing here at this time of day? Shouldn't you be at school?"

He grinned. "I'm taking a personal day and thought I'd drop by and say hello."

"A personal day?"

"Yeah, I had some business to take care of." He drew over a stool to the other side of the counter from her and sat down. "So how are you? Did the Ren Faire wear you out?"

She shook her head. "The hours were long but it was fun."

"I went by your booth a few times, but you were never there."

"No one told me."

"Once I saw you weren't there, I didn't stop."

An odd chill skipped down her spine. Why should his statement cause such a reaction? she wondered. "You should have stopped and said hi. Archie and the others all pitched in and helped me out. That way I was able to keep both the booth and the shop going."

"Was business good?"

"It was excellent."

"I'm glad to hear it. So, what else have you been doing lately? Oh, did you hear about . . ."

She tuned his words out and eyed him reflectively. They'd dated for a while, and it had been fun at first. But several months back he'd started getting too serious, even going so far as to ask her to marry him. She'd tried more than once to break up with him, but nothing she did or said seemed to get through to him. Finally she'd had to use what she considered to be extreme measures. After that he'd made himself scarce.

She'd breathed a sigh of relief, but now she wondered if it was possible that he'd been harboring some anger and resentment toward her all this time. Could he have done the things in her home? He was an expert with tools. Her locks would be child's play to him. . . .

"Hey," he said, laughing good-naturedly. "You aren't paying attention to me."

"I'm sorry. Dennis, are you angry at me because I stopped dating you?"

He looked at her in surprise. "What made you ask that?"

"I don't know. I've been thinking and, well, I was sort of abrupt with you."

He laughed shortly. "To put it mildly. I came to pick you up for dinner one night and found a note stuck to your door, very brief and to the point. It said, *I will not see you anymore.* I couldn't get you to answer the door that night, and you wouldn't pick up the phone—"

"I wasn't there. I had gone to visit my mom."

"So you said later. Annie, I was crazy in love with you. Don't you think I deserved an explanation?"

She sighed. "I'm sorry. I know I mishandled the whole thing, but, Dennis, I *had* tried to tell you before."

He eyed her broodingly. "You're saying I wouldn't listen?"

"That's exactly what I'm saying. With the note, you finally got the message." She gazed at him earnestly. "Dennis, I understand why you would be angry with me."

"Angry?" He ran his hand around the back of his neck. "I don't know. At the time I was hurt more than anything, but I've gotten over it." He chuckled, a forced sound. "In fact I've started dating again—a teacher who works at my school."

"Really? That's wonderful."

He nodded. "So you don't have to worry about me sitting at home, pining for you."

Her headache was getting worse. "I wasn't worrying. I never thought—"

"It's okay." He reached out for her hand. "I'd have loved for things to work out with you and me, Annie, but it didn't and I'm fine with that. Okay? Can we still be friends?"

"Sure. I'd like that." His smile was warm, just as his

hands on hers were. It couldn't be him, she thought. He was dating someone else. But then maybe it was all a screen. Once again she felt a chill.

His watchful gaze slowly narrowed on her. "Is something wrong, Annie? You can tell me if there is."

At the moment the main thing wrong was *her*, she reflected. She had mentally pegged Dennis as a bad guy without one shred of evidence, a man who'd never been anything but nice to her. And knowing all that, she still had doubts at the back of her mind. She was thinking of telling him about some of the things that had been happening at her home to see what his reaction would be, when she spied a customer who needed help. "Excuse me for a minute."

Wyatt left the hardware store with the apologies of the owner ringing in his ears. There were no cell phones to be had anywhere in the town, the owner had assured him. Nevertheless, he glanced up and down Main Street, hoping to find a store that might have one. There was a pharmacy, a produce market next to a meat market, a Debbie's Dress Shop, and a florist. On the other side of the street, he saw an insurance agency, a Bertha's Café, a resale shop, a gift shop, and . . . A smile broke out over his face—and Annie's Place. He crossed the street.

Annie's Place was in an old Victorian house with gingerbread trim and flowers all around. Once inside he saw elegant curtains blowing outward from the windows and double-wide doors that opened into other rooms. Then he saw her.

She was quietly talking to a man who sat on a stool in front of an oak counter. She wasn't wearing a dress made in a style from another time, nor did a coronet of flowers circle her head. She was dressed in jeans, T-shirt, and sandals.

He'd found Annie.

She hadn't noticed him yet and as he drew near her he heard her say, "Something's been happening that I want to talk to you about."

"Annie?"

She started and turned her head. "*Wyatt*. I didn't hear you come in."

"Sorry. I didn't mean to sneak up on you."

"How did you find me?"

"Were you hiding?"

"Of course not, but . . . It's just that I hadn't expected to see you again."

"No?" The close-fitting T-shirt hugged her firm breasts, and the soft-looking jeans invited his gaze to her narrow waist, then downward over her slim hips and long legs to the hot pink, painted toenails peeking out from brown sandals. His mouth went dry.

Last night's moonlight and mist had seemed to wrap her in beauty, but in the bright light of day he could see that beauty hadn't been an illusion. In fact he could see even more loveliness. Like the way various shades of blond and gold sliced through her hair, like the dusting of freckles that covered her nose and part of her cheeks, like the lip gloss that made her lips look soft and kissable.

From the moment he'd walked into her shop and seen her, his body had reacted, heating with urgent need, and he'd wanted to kiss and touch her as he had last night. Actually *more* than he had last night. It was easy to figure out that having a little of Annie wasn't going to be enough for him.

But amazingly the shadows he saw in the depths of her eyes stopped him and instead made him want to pull her close and protect her. From what? he wondered.

She seemed to gather herself together. "I'm sorry. Dennis, this is Wyatt Damaron. He's here visiting Scott. Wyatt, this is my friend Dennis Patterson. He teaches at the high school in the next town. The school serves several towns, including ours."

Wyatt nodded to the man, who seemed annoyed at the interruption. "Nice to meet you."

"Likewise," Dennis said. "You up here for a little fishing?"

"If Scott ever comes back."

That brought an understanding grin from Dennis. "I've got to get going, Annie, but I'll call you later so we can finish our talk."

Watching the interchange, Wyatt thought he saw something more than friendliness in Dennis's gaze as he looked at Annie. Could it be that Dennis was in love with her? If so, he didn't blame him one bit. But the more important question was whether Annie was in love with Dennis. Somehow he didn't think so.

Wyatt waited until Dennis left. "Are you two an item?"

A shake of her head sent her hair swishing over her shoulders. "We're just casual friends."

"Okay, next question. Is something wrong?"

Startled, she looked up at him. "What made you ask a thing like that?"

"Just an impression."

Her gaze shifted to the shop's front door, as if she half expected Dennis to come back. "Well, it's an erroneous impression. There's not a thing wrong."

"Annie, if you've got a problem, I can help."

Her gaze returned to him. "You sound so sure of your abilities."

"I am."

"Of course you are." Suddenly she flashed him a quick grin and the shadows in her eyes vanished. "So, Wyatt Damaron, what's brought you to town today?"

"My cell phone died. You wouldn't happen to have one I could buy, would you?"

"I'm afraid that's one thing I don't sell."

"Would any other place in town carry one?"

"Nope. This just isn't a cell phone kind of town. You may have to fly back to your eastern kingdom to get another."

It was the first sign of the mischievous Lady Anne he'd met the night before. He realized he was relaxing and he hadn't even been aware that he was uptight. "Or maybe I'll just have someone pop one in a package and express it to me."

Her eyes twinkling, she shrugged. "I suppose you

could do that too. You can, that is, if you can find a telephone to use to call and ask that someone to do it."

His brows drew together. "This town must have telephones. All towns, no matter how small, have telephones."

"Is that so?" She shrugged again. "Well then, who knows? Perhaps the many rooms of my castle might hold one."

He remembered, then, that Scott had called her to give her the message for him. She was teasing him, as naturally as if he were the boy next door, just as she had the night before. There were a few of his friends and a host of his enemies who would call her foolish. He would call her disarming and *very* desirable. "Do you have one?"

She waved her hand toward a room at the back of the house. "Help yourself. It's in the office."

He stayed where he was. "Tell me, is it just me?"

"Pardon?" she asked blankly.

Slipping his hands into his trouser pockets, he spread his legs in a wider stance, as if, Annie thought, he were trying to balance himself. "Is it just me you like to tease or do you tease everyone?"

Apparently not many people teased him, and, Annie decided, she could understand why they didn't. Wyatt Damaron carried himself with the self-assurance of a man accustomed to people stepping aside for him, someone with whom most people would be extremely cautious. Scott had laughingly referred to him as ruthless. She didn't know about that, but from what little she'd been able to ascertain about him, he was an Armani-clad stick of dynamite.

"I'll stop the teasing if it bothers you."

"I didn't say that."

"No, but if you weren't bothered by it you wouldn't have brought it up."

"I brought it up because I wanted to know if I was one of many you tease."

She chuckled. "Calm yourself, Wyatt. I'm sure no one would ever mistake you for 'one of many.' "

"You're doing it again," he said softly.

She laughed. "Yes, I am." In the daylight she could see that his lashes were so thick, they intensified the dark smudges beneath his eyes. The laughter faded from her face. "Listen, don't worry. You'll get through all this without too much personal trauma. Scott will be back soon."

His brows rose. "Personal trauma?"

She smiled. "The trauma of being bored."

"I'm never bored."

"My mistake," she said lightly, though her tone clearly said otherwise.

A slow smile spread across his face, a smile that warmed her through her middle. "So tell me about your shop—Annie's Place."

"I sell the works of our local artists and crafts people, along with many other things. Generally I run it by myself during the week, but Harley, who you met last night, comes in most afternoons after school, and on the weekends the artists like to rotate to help out. It's a good arrangement because the customers get to meet the person who created what they're buying."

"It's very nice," he said, wandering around the room, his gaze touching on the pottery, glass vases, and bottles, though he didn't linger over any one thing.

She understood why he wouldn't be interested in the rough-hewn birdhouses, wreaths, and jewelry, but she thought he might have enjoyed a few of the paintings. Then again, what was she thinking? Wyatt Damaron could afford old masters. "There are three more rooms."

"The masks," he said, surprising her by walking over to the wall that held seven of them. "They're wonderful." He studied them, then reached for one placed off to the side, out of the normal line of vision. It was made of leather stretched over balsa wood and decorated with semiprecious stones, golden koi fish scales, and black cock feathers that glistened with green, silver, ruby, and amethyst. "I like this one."

"Really?" she asked, startled.

"Really."

The mask had been hanging on the wall for months, and in that entire time, not one person had reached for it. But Wyatt had. From the moment it had started to take form beneath her hands, the mask had been very special to her. She'd taken more care than usual in each stroke of her paintbrush and in the placement of each stone, each feather, each scale. The result had been a mask unlike any she had ever created. It had an otherworldly mysticism that she'd never been able to duplicate.

"As it happens that mask is one of my favorites."

His gaze cut to her. "Did you make it?"

"Yes."

"The craftsmanship is exquisite."

"Thank you," she said, genuinely pleased that he liked her work.

"There are only seven here. Are there others elsewhere?"

"I sold several during the faire and there are two or three in another room, but I never have that many on hand. It's something I only do in my spare time."

"That's a pity. You have a real talent."

She smiled. "Thank you again, but if there were too many masks produced they wouldn't be special, now would they?"

"As long as you made them, yes, I think they would be."

She laughed. "You're really wonderful for a girl's ego, but the masks are just something I do because they're fun. If I had to really work at them, they wouldn't be fun anymore."

"Fun?"

"Sure. The masks are pure fantasy."

"That makes sense, since I can personally attest to the fact that you like fantasy."

"Why?" she asked.

"Last night's playacting."

She thought for a moment, but was unable to connect the two things as he had. Finally, she simply shrugged.

His eyes narrowed. "Was last night really that routine to you that you've already forgotten about it? Have there been that many men who you've kissed in the mist, then teased until they didn't know which way was up?"

Last night after she'd found the roses in her bedroom, she hadn't been able to think of too much else. But she hadn't forgotten about him. No woman would be able to. He was too male, too virile, even moody in a strange way.

"If no one else would ever consider you 'one of many,' " she said softly, "then Wyatt, you shouldn't either."

His intense gaze seemed to be trying to penetrate her mind. It was so sharp, she almost took a step backward.

"You know," he said finally, "masks are not only fantasy, they're also made to hide behind. Is there something—or someone—you're hiding from?"

She couldn't help but burst out laughing and was grateful for the release from the tension that had been building between them. "You got that from the fact that I make masks?"

"You didn't?"

"No," she said, wondering at his amazing perception. "No matter how long I thought about it, I probably would never have gotten that." It was the truth. But there was also another truth that she tried hard to keep buried. "Wyatt Damaron, you're a remarkable man."

"Is that a compliment?"

"It's most definitely a compliment, though I doubt you really care one way or the other."

"I wouldn't have asked if I didn't care." His tone was so serious, there was no way she could doubt him. He held up the mask. "Does it have a name?"

"I call it 'The Sorcerer.' "

"Interesting," he murmured. "That's the same thing you called me last night."

She'd completely forgotten about that. Her brow wrinkled at the coincidence. "You know . . . what I said last night . . . it was more about the silver streak in your hair than anything else."

"I know. You were teasing me."

She nodded. Perhaps she *had* been unconsciously thinking about the mask when she'd made the comment, but she seriously doubted it. Still, what were the odds that he'd go straight for the mask she'd named "The Sorcerer"? Even more strange, the black opal eyes she'd created months ago for the mask strongly resembled Wyatt's eyes—both the opals and Wyatt's eyes were so dark, it seemed at times as if they had swallowed the light.

He bent his head to study the mask more closely. His fingers touched it gently, almost reverently. "You really did a beautiful job on this." He handed it to her. "Would you ring it up for me?"

"Oh, I'm sorry. I should have told you right off that it's not for sale." She brushed past him and hung it back on the wall.

His gaze followed her curiously. "If it's not for sale, then why is it displayed?"

"I like to look at it during the day." It was something else she couldn't really explain. "Perhaps you'd like one of the other masks."

"So you're saying all the other masks are for sale?"

"That's right."

"Then it's not that you're reluctant to sell something you've made, but rather you just don't want to part with this particular one. Why?"

She shrugged. "Chalk it up to a personal quirk."

His lips twitched. "I can deal with quirks. In fact I have one myself, which is that I want this mask. Name your price, Annie."

She chuckled good-naturedly. "You can save your steamroller boardroom tactics for when it will do you some good. The mask is not for sale at any price. Besides, you really haven't looked at the others. You may like one of those even better. Come with me, and I'll show you the ones in the other room." She took a few steps, then realized he wasn't following her.

"When I find something I want," he said gently, "I don't usually look any further."

Thoroughly enjoying the exchange, she regarded him with amusement. "You're obviously a man who is used to having anything you want, Wyatt, but what you need to understand is that you can't have that particular mask. I advise you to accept the fact and learn to deal with it. Who knows? You may even become a better man for it."

He smiled. "I do understand a reluctance to part with something that is yours. Actually I feel the same way."

Possessiveness. Yes, she thought, a man like Wyatt Damaron would definitely be possessive. An interesting trait, she supposed. But she wondered if he'd had something particular in mind when he'd made the statement. Was it a piece of property? A company? A business? A person? She began to wonder what kind of person would bring out the possessiveness in him, and she went with the thought. "Could I interest you in a piece of jewelry for your wife or girlfriend?"

His gaze held steady on her. "You probably could if I had either, but I don't. And don't worry, I won't keep trying to buy the mask if you don't want to sell it." He took out a business card, flipped it over, and wrote a number on it. "I would appreciate it, however, if you would notify me if you ever change your mind about it."

She looked down at the card he'd handed her. "Just out of curiosity, who would answer this phone if I did happen to call?"

"Someone who has access to me twenty-four hours a day."

What a staggering thought, she reflected wryly. To have that kind of access to a man like Wyatt would require stamina, devotion, and nerves of steel. She slipped the card into her jeans.

"Wait a minute," he said, an unreadable expression in his eyes. "May I have that card back?"

"Sure." She handed it to him and watched while he wrote down another number.

"There. That's my personal cell phone number.

Now, after I receive my new phone tomorrow, you can reach *me* at any time."

She looked down at the card, then back at him. "Why do you want the mask so badly?"

"There's just something about it that appeals to me."

She nodded, accepting his explanation without further question. She understood how a piece of art, for whatever reason, could reach out and touch a person. "I promise that if I ever decide to sell the mask, I'll sell it to you."

"Thank you."

Wyatt was like a dose of adrenaline, she reflected. She'd only been with him a short time, yet her senses were vibrantly alive. But much as she'd enjoyed it, she had responsibilities. "Excuse me. I need to go help those people over there. Help yourself to the phone. And if you see anything else you like, bring it to me and I'll ring it up for you."

"Thanks," he said. "I will."

Feeling his gaze on her as she walked away, she smiled to herself. Who knew what he was thinking? She'd never know. It would take too much time and too much effort to find out. Unfortunate, maybe, but it was better for her to accept him at face value—a man who was Scott's friend and who wouldn't be in town long.

One good thing—sparring with him had made her headache disappear.

❖————————❖

Annie waved good-bye to a customer who had just bought a unique weather vane. A couple of hours had passed since Wyatt had disappeared toward her office. Every time she'd started to check on him another customer had showed up. But now she finally had a few moments.

She found him sitting behind her paper-strewn desk. "Are you through with the phone?"

He nodded, closing a mystery novel that she recognized as one from her office bookshelf. "As a thank-you for letting me use your phone, I'd like to take you out to dinner tonight."

"No thanks are necessary," she said with a dismissive wave of her hand.

"Okay, then. Have dinner with me to make up for the fact that you won't let me buy your mask."

She laughed. "You really aren't going to drop that, are you?"

Smiling, he lifted a letter opener and twirled it between two fingers. "Sure I am. I'm trying to get over my disappointment even as we speak. But I feel I may need a little help. So, Annie, would you please be so kind as to help me learn to *deal* with it—as you so charmingly put it—and go out with me tonight?"

"No, thank you."

He dropped the letter opener. "Not going to buy that, huh? Okay, then how about this. Have dinner with me because I want you to . . . and because you want to."

"You're very sure of yourself."

His smile widened. "You're saying that as if it isn't a good thing."

Habit rather than pain had her briefly pressing her fingers against the center of her forehead. "Look, Wyatt, let's be truthful. You're just killing time until Scott gets back and, quite frankly, I don't like killing time."

"What if I promise you that having dinner with me tonight would not be killing time?"

"What do you mean?" She waited, amused and expectant, knowing he'd come up with something good.

"What if I showed you something truly amazing tonight? Would you consider that to be wasting time?"

"I don't know. What would you show me?"

"You're going to have to come and see."

She smiled. "With all your money I'm sure you could show me loads of amazing things. Let me see if I can guess what you have in mind. Ummm—okay. You're going to gas up one of your jets and fly us to France for dinner on top of the Eiffel Tower. Or perhaps use your influence to open the Tower of London and show me the crown jewels. No, wait a minute, I know—you plan to dazzle me by buying me one or two of the pieces."

He pushed up from the chair and walked around the desk to her. "Are any of those things something you'd like to have happen?"

Seeing that he was half serious, she had to laugh. "No."

His expression was completely enigmatic. "Then no, you guessed wrong. I have something much simpler in mind."

"*Whoa.* Let me get this straight. You mean you're proposing to dazzle me *without* using your wealth and influence?"

His brows rose, and a glint came into his eyes. "You don't think I can?"

"I don't really know."

"Well there's only one way you'll find out, now isn't there?" He reached out and touched her hair with the same care he'd used to touch the mask. "Come on, Annie. Have a little faith. Give me a chance."

He couldn't have done a better job of intriguing her if he'd really put out an effort, she reflected, and he hadn't. He'd simply brought all his persuasive powers to bear and refused to take no for an answer. It was an ability he'd probably been born with. And the fact remained that he *had* intrigued her.

She grinned. "So what are you going to do? Perform feats of magic?"

"Come out with me tonight, Annie."

Feeling as if she were about to dive into deep water, she drew in a long breath. "All right, Wyatt Damaron. I'll go out with you tonight. As it happens, I'm very much in the mood to be dazzled and amazed."

He looked at her for what seemed to her to be a very long time, but in reality was only moments. "What's your last name?"

"Logan."

"Annie Logan," he murmured.

A smile spread slowly across his face, so bright and self-assured, she almost closed her eyes against the force of it. She didn't, though, because she had the very sure feeling she'd regret it if she missed one second of the experience of Wyatt Damaron.

"Then, Annie Logan," he said softly, seductively, "I'll do my best."

THREE

What would dazzle and amaze Annie? He only knew what wouldn't. The Eiffel Tower and the crown jewels were definitely out. Wyatt smiled to himself. Any other woman would go crazy over either of those things, but not Annie.

He was grateful to Scott, he decided. If his friend had been on time, he might never have met Annie Logan.

Annie.

There wasn't an artificial bone in her body. Best of all she knew exactly who he was yet she didn't feel intimidated or impressed. She was unaffected, spontaneous, and delightful. In many ways, she seemed almost untouched by the world. And when he left there, he'd like to remember her that way—without the imprint of the world on her. Or the imprint of him.

She had him warring with himself. He had a deep, abiding need to make her his, if only for a little while.

But he was also fighting against the unexpected need to protect her, even if it was from himself. He saw her as one of nature's creations that would be changed forever if touched, like a delicate piece of coral still growing beneath the sea.

And he was having a hell of a hard time believing that he was actually thinking that way.

She lived next door to her shop, in a Victorian house, equally as charming as Annie's Place, though smaller. He'd barely knocked on the door when she opened it. And when she smiled up at him, he knew his good intentions of not touching her were in big trouble.

She wore a scoop-necked, yellow-and-cream-flowered dress that fell to her ankles. Her hair gleamed brightly, and her eyes glittered with friendliness. The only piece of jewelry she wore was a locket that hung on a thin gold chain around her neck and nestled in the cleavage of her breast.

"Come in," she said, stepping aside.

"Thank you." Her home, he saw, was a warm, welcoming place furnished in whites and ivories with soft textures that enticed, comfortable cushions that invited, and sheer voile curtains that undulated sensually on the night breeze. Her home was just like she was, he thought hazily.

She looked up at him, her expression uncertain. "Since I have no idea what we're going to do tonight, I didn't know how to dress."

"You dressed perfectly," he said thickly, "and you look beautiful."

She dropped a little curtsy. "Thank you, Sir Wyatt of Damaron."

One second he was looking at her, the next he was pulling her into his arms. He hadn't known he was going to do it, and once it happened he hadn't been able to stop himself. After one small start of surprise, she yielded, her lips parting beneath his, her tongue thrusting upward into his mouth to meet his. She melted into him, returning the pressure of his kisses, their intensity, their heat, then creating her own demands.

Her uninhibited response was like a dream to him. He drew her closer, crushing her against his chest. She moaned into his mouth and with a rough groan he swallowed the sound.

Her natural sensuality overwhelmed him. Her innate fire clouded his mind. She was all woman, curves and fullness, warmth and desire, and she didn't hold anything back. He'd never known a woman to respond so quickly, so easily, so freely. He was astonished and ecstatic. He ached all over for her.

In frustration he plunged his tongue deeper into her mouth, but it was a pale imitation of what he really wanted to do to her, with her.

Standing on her tiptoes, she wrapped her arms around his neck and held on tightly. An almost unbearable tension built and coiled in him. A shudder raced through him as he kissed her again. How in God's name was he supposed to resist her?

But he had to, he reminded himself. To save her. And in an odd, nebulous way that he wasn't yet sure of, to save himself.

Slowly, he drew away from her. Then with a slightly trembling hand, he brushed delicate strands of her hair away from her face. Her lips were swollen and moist. Her eyes were misty, her skin flushed, her breathing uneven. And he knew that if he looked in the mirror he would see the very same things.

She ran her tongue around her mouth. "Congratulations, Wyatt," she whispered. "That's an *amazing* way to start off the evening."

The need to pull her back into his arms slammed into him with such force that for a moment he couldn't breathe. But to protect her, to protect himself, he instead tilted back his head and laughed.

Annie sighed with contentment, stretched her legs out in front of her, and leaned back on her hands. "You know, I never would have guessed you were a campfire kind of guy," she said with an easy grin, as a cool wind ruffled through her hair. "It's a great campfire."

He smiled at her. "I'm glad my efforts meet with your approval."

"They most certainly do."

They sat on a high knoll in the middle of a glade, a blanket beneath them, a wide, black sky stretching to infinity above them. Majestic firs and noble hemlocks etched their shapes against the sky. The campfire he'd built crackled before them, its flames red, gold, and orange.

"And by the way, congratulations again. You've totally dazzled and amazed me with this elegant dinner you managed to get out of Bertha. Obviously you cast some sort of magic spell over her. The cooking at Bertha's Café usually runs the gamut from fried to deep-fried, but our dinner was *wonderful*. And who knew she kept champagne on hand?" She took a sip from her goblet. "Plus—and this may be the most amazing part, she put it all together for you in a basket and allowed you to leave the premises with it. She *heartily* dislikes any form of takeout and has always refused to do it."

"Really?" he said as he finished putting the last of their dishes back into the basket. "Well, Bertha couldn't have been more helpful. She even threw in extras like the blankets and the lantern."

"Helpful? Obviously my mistake with her has been that I'm not a fabulous-looking, charming man with a pair of amazingly seductive eyes." Somewhat perplexed, he looked at her and she laughed. "Oh, come on. You know it as well as I do."

His lips twitched. "Actually I've never heard anyone put it that way."

"Anyone? You mean women, right?" She shrugged. "They probably used other words, but trust me, the meaning was more than likely the same."

He shifted closer to her so that he could see her every expression and inhale the light, sensual scent that came from her skin. "You know what?"

"What?"

"You manage to dazzle me every time you speak."

She tilted her head to one side. "Aren't you used to the truth?"

"Sure, I am. But, other than from my family, truths

put differently, even twisted at times, and definitely with more nuances than the ones you tell me."

"That's a funny way to put it."

"Your truths are pure, Annie. I don't need a shovel or a search team to find the meaning in them."

She crossed her ankles. "You must keep interesting company if you have to do that with your other friends."

His smile was enigmatic. "So tell me another truth."

"What do you want to know?"

He leaned back on one elbow until he was on his side, facing her. "To start with, I want to know why, both times I've kissed you, you've responded completely and naturally and with enough fire to drive me crazy."

Her expression turned curious. "Is that a complaint?"

"No *way*, no *how*." Driven by a compulsion he didn't bother to try to control, he raised up and pressed a brief kiss to her lips, then relaxed back on his elbow. "But with the first few kisses, most women are tentative and don't really respond completely until after they've gotten to know a man better."

"Is that so?" she asked, truly interested. "You sound very experienced."

"Don't change the subject."

"Well, what can I say? Given your analysis of kisses, I suppose my response to them puts me squarely in the 'Shameless Hussy' category."

He shook his head firmly. "Trust me. You don't fit into any category I know of."

"Maybe not," she said easily, "but you *are* trying to figure me out."

"Yeah, I am," he conceded, "but *trying* is the operative word. Frankly I'm not at all sure it's even possible to figure you out."

"Then why try?" She quickly waved her hand, stopping his answer. "Oh, never mind. All of this because of a kiss. Wyatt, you're thinking too much. The answer to your question is simple. I responded to your kiss as I did, because I liked the way you were kissing me and the way it made me feel. It was . . . amazing."

She blew him away. When he'd used the words *unsure* and *tentative* to describe how most women responded to first kisses, he'd been shielding her from the more harsh, but accurate words—*calculatingly coy.*

But not Annie. She was completely without guile. She wouldn't keep a man waiting when he knocked on her door. She wouldn't know how to play games, doling out treats a little at a time in order to hook him.

"So how on earth did you ever find this place?" she asked in a tone that told him her mind had wandered.

He'd never met a woman whose mind would wander if she were the topic of conversation. Astounding. "Bertha again. She gave me detailed instructions, along with a map."

"Sometimes I backpack up here, but I go another way. It's great here and, by the way, very unexpected. I was sure you were going to conjure up a five-star dinner by flying in a world-class chef from somewhere."

"Good idea. Maybe next time."

She sat her champagne flute down on the ground,

picked up a pinecone, and tossed it into the fire, causing the flames to turn blue, then red. "Not for me, thanks, but you can keep it in mind for another time, and another woman."

At the moment he couldn't comprehend ever being with another woman again, but he would be. There'd always been another. When he had time, that was.

But there was Annie now, an Annie that riveted him with her warmth and ease, and unconsciously seductive ways. She could make a man forget all other women and engross him for a lifetime. "Do you always say what you're thinking?"

Her brow wrinkled. "More analysis, Wyatt?"

"Bear with me. I really want to know."

She sighed, and combed her fingers through her hair. The motion stretched the material of her dress taut against her breast. Warmth slipped into his bloodstream.

She gestured vaguely. "Okay, well, I guess it depends on the circumstances and my mood."

He fingered the corner of her skirt, a flowing fabric that had touched her skin and picked up her scent. "Then what mood were you in last night?"

She tensed slightly. "Last night?"

"You don't remember?"

"A lot happened last night." The roses. God, the roses. "Give me a clue."

"Last night you said you could easily fall in love with a man like me if you were the kind of woman who fell in love."

The tension eased away, and with a grin, she rolled

her eyes. "Uh-oh. I'm doomed. One more thing that puts me in the 'Shameless Hussy' category."

"Actually it puts you in a category called Annie," he said with a soft smile, "a category that's mind-blowing."

She grimaced. "Well, I'm sorry about the remark if it bothered you, and I certainly didn't mean to get you thinking any more than you already do. It was just a thought I had at the time, and I thought I'd tell you. You're a fantastic man, Wyatt. No news there. Most women who were lucky enough to have you float into their life would fall in love with you in an instant."

"Most?"

"Sure. Those who weren't already involved with someone."

He chuckled. "You certainly have an interesting view of me."

She studied him. "That remark really does bother you."

His lips curled wryly. "Let me put it this way. I just thought it was an interesting thing for you to say."

"Well, it's certainly nothing for you to be bothered over. You're definitely the kind of man women lose their hearts over, but I'm not telling you anything there you don't already know. As for me, it's simple. I can't imagine ever falling in love."

"Why not? Because you've never been in love?"

"Right, I haven't." Staring at the fire, she thought for a moment. "Maybe it's because I've been so busy."

"Doing what?"

She looked at him. "Living."

"I should have known."

"It's the truth."

He chuckled. "Oh, I never doubted it."

"You know, I've never really thought about it too much, but I just don't think I'm interested in love. After all, life is so short and love can be constricting in many ways." She brushed a strand of her hair off her face and looked at him. "How about you? Have you ever been in love?"

"No."

"Well, then, there you are. We may be more alike than we thought."

He burst out laughing. "No, Annie, I'm not like you. In my experience, no one is."

She eyed him thoughtfully, then shrugged. "Okay."

"Okay what?"

"Okay, you're not like me." She picked up her champagne glass and handed it to him. "I've had plenty, thank you."

Clearly, she had once again tired of being the topic of conversation, he thought as he put her glass away with his, then looked back at her. One side of her face was in light, the other side in shadow. To him she was as mysterious on the inside as she looked at that moment. "Are you cold?"

"A little."

He unfolded another blanket and draped it around her shoulders like a shawl.

"Bertha?" she asked, her lips curving in amusement.

"She told me we'd need the extra blankets."

"She was right," she said, staring up at the sky. "It's very dark tonight."

Once again her thoughts had drifted and he wondered where they'd gone. "I was hoping the stars would be out in full force. I figured that would help with the dazzle category."

"A dark sky is just as interesting," she said softly. "It has its moods. You just have to study it."

Her gaze was on the sky, his was on her. "I'd rather study you." He lightly skimmed the back of his fingers down her cheek.

She looked over at him. "No more analysis, Wyatt. I'm not that complicated."

"If you say so."

"I do. So what's next?"

A bright smile crossed her face and just like that she was back with him.

"Do you have something else planned to dazzle and amaze me? Any feats of magic up your sleeve?"

If he kissed her right then, there would be plenty of sparks, all kinds of magic, and never-ending fireworks, but he was still fighting against himself. He had an almost overwhelming urge to draw her to him and touch her in every way there was. But there was still that part of him that didn't want to alter something so perfect. "Let me first say that I have nothing planned. I'm winging the whole evening."

With a mischievous smile, she dipped her head in regal approval. "You wing pretty well, Sir Wyatt of Damaron."

His pulse jumped, then raced. The things she could do to him with just a smile or a nod of her head were remarkable. "Thank you."

"So wing something else."

He grinned. "Why do I feel that's a challenge?"

"Maybe because it is."

He looked around him. "Let me see. . . . Maybe I do have something." He stood and disappeared in the direction of the car. Minutes later he was back with a silver blanket. With a flourish he unfurled it over the fire, then let it settle over the flames. Within moments the fire-retardant material had extinguished the fire, leaving only glowing embers that shimmered and changed colors with the wafting breeze.

As if she were a little girl at a birthday party, Annie clapped delightedly. "Wonderful, wonderful."

He gave a courtier's bow, then dropped down to her side. "Bertha again. She drilled fire safety into me."

"That's our Bertha."

"Of course now I've blown my one magic act and in the process taken away our warmth."

"No problem. We've got a blanket." She held out one side. "Want to join me?" He hesitated, and she laughed. "I promise I'll try not to do anything shameless. Or am I being shameless just by asking you to join me?"

Darkness surrounded her, he reflected. The warmth and light of the fire were gone. She was out in the middle of nowhere with a man who wanted her more and more with every beat of his heart. He was tired of holding back. With one more touch he might change her. With one more kiss he could make her his.

He shifted his body against hers and adjusted the blanket around both their shoulders.

"Now that I've got you here," she said with a grin, "what on earth am I going to do with you?"

"You're teasing me again." His voice was deep and husky.

"Shamelessly, I'm afraid." She laughed. "See? That settles it. I *am* a Shameless Hussy. I wonder if there's a twelve-step program for people like me. What do you think?"

He turned to her. "I think you shouldn't tease me," he said gruffly. "Not right now—"

"*Oh! Look!*" She pointed toward the sky. "A shooting star!"

His mind was clouded with her scent, the feel of her body against his. "A what?"

"There's *another*," she said breathlessly. "And another. What's happening?"

"I—"

"You know what? I think it's a meteor shower. *Wyatt!* It's a meteor shower!" Her eyes were glistening with wonderment. "This is why you brought me up here, isn't it? You knew!"

His mind was clearing now. "No. At least I don't think I—"

She laughed. "You said if I came tonight my time wouldn't be wasted. You're wonderful, Wyatt. You've truly dazzled and amazed me." She lay down on her back, and with a hand on his shoulder, urged him down beside her.

He gladly complied, and for over an hour he was as dazzled as she. One after another, shooting stars streamed across the black velvet sky. Sometimes there were long, brilliant streaks of light. Other times, three would come at one time. Then once in a while there would be seconds or minutes between them. Occasionally there'd be an explosion where one would break apart into little sparks, first white, then as it faded, blue. There was no sound except for Annie's soft exclamations.

And when the heavens closed up again, he rolled over onto his side so that he could see her, another heavenly constellation as far as he was concerned.

"You really are a magic man," she whispered.

His urgency to have her had been eased by the splendor they had witnessed, but still he couldn't resist her. He kissed her softly and with the same awe he'd had for the meteor shower. For another night at least, she'd go untouched. It was all he could promise himself.

Wyatt was fire, there was no doubt about it.

As Annie settled in amid the pillows on her bed, thoughts of the preceding hours she'd spent with him came swirling back to her.

Wyatt was a powerfully compelling, highly sensual man who was trying to figure her out, trying to understand what it was about her that attracted him to her.

Frankly she was surprised he hadn't figured it out yet, because the answer wasn't at all complicated. It was the same reason she was attracted to him. *Chemistry.*

The chemistry the two of them had together was strong enough to rearrange the Rockies. But by all accounts the Rockies were perfectly fine the way they were now and so was she.

She obviously had a decision to make.

From their very first kiss, she'd known they could create fire together. She'd also been aware of the sexual tension that simmered just beneath the surface of every look, every touch, and every word they exchanged.

But she wasn't afraid of falling in love with him, nor was she afraid of being hurt. She had sense enough to know that making love to a man like Wyatt would not be an ordinary thing. Her world might shift, her reason might flee, but it would all be temporary, and in the end, she would still be the same woman, with the same happy life she'd made for herself, and the same dark secrets she had to keep.

She knew better than anyone how fleeting and fragile life was. She'd learned to make each moment the best that she could, and then go on without regret.

So when the time came for her to make the decision, and it *would* come, she would simply do as she'd always done. She would do what felt right.

FOUR

Humming beneath her breath, Annie switched a blue birdhouse with a red one, then pushed a weather vane to the back of the shelf and filled a cut-glass container with potpourri. She was in an extraordinarily good mood, she mused, but then why shouldn't she be? She'd had a great time with Wyatt the night before. This morning the sun was shining, the day was clear, and she'd already had quite a few people through her shop. She'd even dressed brightly in a flowing, tiered skirt and bustier in lavender, green, and purple. A lavender ribbon laced the bustier up to the neckline, where it tied in a bow.

But the happiest thing of all was that last night when she'd returned home from her date with Wyatt, she'd found nothing disturbed, added, or taken away. She chose to take it as a good sign.

The mischief at her home had started shortly after the Ren Faire people had arrived and the roses had appeared during their last night in town. The timing suggested that the person who'd been doing it might have been with the faire. She supposed it could have even been one of her friends who thought it was a great joke. It definitely hadn't been a joke to her, but then the person would have no way of knowing that.

But she still had unanswered questions. For instance, why would one of her friends do such things? And if it had been one of her friends, why hadn't he told her before he left and had the satisfaction of seeing her reaction firsthand?

This new theory of hers didn't make perfect sense, but there was one thing about it. If she was right, there should be no more mischief.

On the other hand, if there was . . .

There was one more possibility that she hadn't let herself address. It was too frightening for her to even contemplate. What had saved her so far from having to confront this particular fear was that the things that had happened were the wrong style. Plus there had been no real threats or harm done. So far.

The phone rang, and she jumped. Shaking her head at herself she went to answer it. "Annie's Place."

"Hey, Annie, it's Dennis."

"Hi." Her mind raced to refocus. Why was he calling?

"I'm on a break and I thought I'd give you a ring since we didn't have a chance to finish our talk yesterday."

"Oh . . . right." She'd almost forgotten that she'd

wondered if he could be the prankster. She had a new theory today, but it wouldn't hurt to make sure Dennis understood how she felt about what was going on, just in case.

"I called you several times last night."

She heard a faint hint of accusation in his words. "I was out."

"A date?" he asked, a little too sharply.

She hesitated. "It doesn't matter."

He was silent for a moment. "You went out with Wyatt Damaron, didn't you?"

"Where I was last night has nothing to do with you, Dennis."

"If you say so."

"I do."

"So you said you wanted to talk to me about something?"

"Yes. I wanted to tell you about some funny things that have been happening at my house."

"Funny things? Like what?"

"Like things going missing, pictures rearranged, that sort of thing."

"Okay. So?"

"So I don't like it. Not one little bit." Despite her best efforts, her voice quivered.

"Wait a minute. Are you telling me this because you think *I* did it? Annie, you could have misplaced the things that are missing. As for the pictures, maybe you rearranged them and forgot about it."

"I didn't. I also didn't send myself a bouquet of roses that mysteriously appeared in my bedroom."

"You *do* think I did those things, don't you?"

"I don't know who's responsible, Dennis, and no, I'm not accusing you." He sounded so resentful and hurt that she felt a pang of regret. She'd once considered him a good friend, but of all the people she knew, Dennis had the skills and the best motive to have done those things. Then again, a minute ago she'd been sure it had been someone from the faire. "It's just, well, if you know anything . . ."

"I didn't do any of those things, Annie. I wouldn't."

"I'm sorry if I hurt your feelings, but I've been—unsettled."

"Have you contacted the sheriff?"

"You know as well as I do that the sheriff would file my complaint in the trash. He thinks anyone connected with the faire, not to mention the arts and crafts people around here, is already suspect."

Dennis snorted. "Too bad he's not ready to retire."

"Yeah, I know."

"Look, let me help you. I can fix your locks so that *no* one can get in, and while I'm at it, maybe I can get to the bottom of this and find out who's responsible. I can come over in the evenings and—"

Her hand tightened on the receiver. "No, that's not necessary."

"Maybe not, but I want to help you."

She remembered wondering if whoever was responsible wanted her to reach out to them for help. "I appreciate it, but nothing happened last night while I was out, and I'm hoping that means the pranks have stopped."

"But what if they haven't?"

Unexpectedly a shudder racked through her. Had there been something ominous in his voice, or was she simply hearing things that really weren't there? "I'm sure that they have."

"Okay, then. But just remember I'm here for you. Call me any time day or night and I'll come running."

"Thanks, Dennis. Good-bye."

She replaced the receiver in its cradle and stared at it thoughtfully. Dennis was very eager to help her. Despite the fact that he had begun to date someone else, he obviously still cared for her, perhaps more than just as a friend. Was her initial suspicion right? Could he be the culprit?

"Annie?"

Startled, she whirled around, a hand pressed to her breast. "*Wyatt!* I didn't hear you come in." Almost unconsciously she took in a deep breath and made sure both her feet were planted firmly on the floor. She felt a need to be rooted and centered with Wyatt there in front of her, as if she might be swept away by his dark good looks and disarming eyes.

"You were on the phone, and it sounded like a pretty intense conversation. I didn't want to bother you."

She gave a vague wave of her hand. "Oh, it wasn't anything important. I was just talking to Dennis. Remember him? You met him yesterday."

He nodded. "I remember."

Since she'd known Wyatt, she'd seen him in nothing but cashmere sweaters and tailored slacks. But today he wore a sport jacket and shirt with jeans. Rugged elegance. Before now she hadn't realized there could be such a style.

She'd learned all that was soft about Wyatt ended with his clothes. He might move through the world with easy charm, but scratch the man and you'd find pure steel. She was very aware that by teasing him, she was taunting a sorcerer, and he'd take it only as long as it suited him. When it didn't, he'd vanish in a flash on a big silver bird.

She wasn't one of those people who thrived on danger. She didn't like anything about it, not the icy dread in her stomach or the cold rush of fear through her body. But even though she knew Wyatt had the potential to be dangerous in ways she couldn't even begin to imagine, she wasn't afraid of him. He made her curious. She wanted to see how long it would be before he decided to return to his own life, or if she would be the one to back away. She also wanted to see how much she could scratch before she found the steel.

And now he was frowning at her. "Is something wrong? I heard you say something about pranks."

"Oh, it was nothing serious." The last thing she wanted was to get Wyatt involved.

"If it isn't serious, why did you *sound* so serious?"

"As I told Dennis, someone's been pulling a few pranks at my house, but I think it's over now."

"Pranks?"

"Innocent stuff." True enough, she supposed.

"But you don't know who's been doing it?"

She shook her head. "It's not important." She

searched her mind for something that would get him off
the subject. "Is Scott back yet?"

"No."

He was still staring at her, his brows knitted.

She persevered. "Well, it's got to be something important for him to miss this time with you."

His lips twitched. "It's probably a woman."

She grinned, relieved that he'd finally accepted the
change of subject. "There's no telling. So what are you
going to do? Hang around and hope he shows up soon,
or return home?"

"I'm going to stay a little while longer," he said.
"Maybe do some fishing."

Her heart lightened. She was never bored, but she
had to admit that having Wyatt around made things
incredibly interesting. "Wanda's Bait and Party Shop
on the edge of town should be able to fix you up with
anything you need."

"Thanks. I'll remember that."

"Oh, and if you stay for a few more days, you'll get
to attend the annual Autumn Fest. Normally there's a
month between the Ren Faire and our Autumn Fest,
but this year's Ren Faire schedule got screwed up and
they arrived late." She shrugged. "Since our Autumn
Fest is always scheduled in September on the night of
the full moon, we really couldn't change our schedule
even if we wanted to." He was frowning at her as if he
didn't understand. "Our Autumn Fest is totally different from the Ren Faire. The fest is just for our town
and the surrounding area. Each year we raise money for
different things, and this year, it's for our library."

He was still frowning. "But it's not officially autumn yet."

"Oh, we know. But after September, it starts getting cold here, so we take a small amount of license with the calendar. By the way, have you gotten your cell phone yet?"

"It's out in the car."

"Feel better now that you're connected to the outside world again?" she teased.

He nodded. "But not for the reasons you probably think. My family makes a special effort to keep in touch with one another in case one of us needs something."

"That's really nice. In this day and age families aren't always able to remain close for one reason or another."

His gaze swept the store then returned to her. "Will you go out with me again?"

Excitement zinged through her veins. "When?"

"This afternoon."

She grinned. "In case you haven't noticed, *you're* the one on vacation, not me. I've got the shop to run."

"You could get someone to come in, couldn't you?"

"Probably. If it was for a special enough occasion. What do you have in mind? More magic, I hope?"

He chuckled. "Has anyone ever told you that you're a very demanding woman?"

A couple wandered into the shop, but she ignored them. "Nope."

His eyes glittered with humor. "You may have a hard time believing this, but my dates are usually very content just to be with me."

Annie made a sad face. "How boring for you."

"At least you didn't say how boring for *them*."

"I tell the truth, remember?"

"Oh, I definitely remember."

"So how about it? Is magic on the menu?"

He groaned good-naturedly. "You're not going to give me a break, are you?"

She shrugged, playfully nonchalant. "If it's too much for you, just say the word. If you're not up for the challenge . . ."

With a wide grin on his face, he slowly shook his head. "You really are incorrigible. Fortunately this morning I am up to it." He reached out his hand to her ear and withdrew a silver coin.

She gasped with delight. "You really are a magic man."

His grin broadened. "When I was eight I had a magic kit that I just about wore out. But you know, I'd forgotten all about my fascination with magic until I met you."

"Well you're a natural. The meteor shower you conjured up last night was spectacular."

"As much as I'd like to take the credit, I had nothing to do with it. I can't decide if I had read about it and the knowledge was tucked away somewhere in the back of my mind, or whether I just got lucky."

She held up her hand. "No, no, don't say that. I don't want my illusions ruined." She clasped her hands together and rolled up on her toes, then back on her heels, like a child full of anticipation and expectations.

She hadn't felt like this in a very long time. "Tell me all about your kit. Do you still have it?"

"I haven't seen that thing in years. It may be up in the attic, or it could have been thrown out, for all I know. But it was a great kit, just perfect for an aspiring eight-year-old magician. I had a cape and everything, and I used to drive my family crazy with my practicing. Actually, looking back, they were all wonderful about it, but my mom was the most cooperative."

The door closed after the couple, and Annie belatedly realized that she hadn't once spoken to them. But with Wyatt's eyes alight with his childhood memories, he was close to irresistible. "Thank heaven God made moms, right?"

"Right," he said with what she thought was a touch of wistfulness, but he went on so quickly, she couldn't be sure. "But even Mom drew the line when I wanted to saw her in half."

"I can understand that."

He smiled down at her. "Maybe you can, but at the time I couldn't. My feelings were really hurt."

"Awww, you poor little boy," she said lightly, still wondering at the wistfulness she thought she'd heard. "So what did your mom do?"

"As I recall she made me feel much better by baking me a batch of chocolate cookies."

She laughed. "Sounds like your mom knew how to create some magic of her own."

"That she did."

Something in his tone—regret, pain—caught her attention. "She *did*?"

A shadow crossed his face. "She and my father were killed in a plane crash a number of years ago."

"Wyatt, I'm so sorry. How awful for you."

He nodded. "Yes, it was, it is. But let's get back to the subject of your going out with me again."

She understood all too well what it was like to lose someone you loved so dearly. She also understood why he didn't want to linger on it. "Okay, back to our date. Do you have something particular in mind?"

"Sort of. How would you feel about going with me in search of gold and silver?"

"Gold and silver?" She frowned. "Has someone told you there are mines up here? Maybe there are, but I've never heard of any, at least not right around here."

"I didn't say anything about mines, now did I? I simply asked if you would like to go in search of gold and silver with me."

She snapped her fingers. "Oh, wait a minute. Did someone slip you a map of a long-lost mine? You know, like the legendary Lost Dutchman's mine?"

He chuckled. "Now who's thinking too hard? No, I assure you I'm thinking of something much less foolish and hopefully a little more romantic."

"Boy, do you ever know how to hook a girl." She stared at him in amazement. "No wonder women fall all over themselves when you're around."

He sighed, and shook his head. "Let me guess. Scott, right?"

"Never mind." She waved her hand back and forth as if she were erasing the words from the air. "Tell me about the magic. If I go out with you this afternoon, will there be any involved? Because it would be really wonderful if there was."

"You're a tough audience, Annie Logan. You want magic on demand, but true magic is only magic if it's spontaneous."

Who would have known that the hard, worldly Wyatt Damaron would have such specific views on magic? she reflected with wonder. As for herself, she didn't even know why she kept at him about the magic. She was going to go out with him. Saying no wasn't even an option. "Okay, but tell me something. This spontaneous magic—will it involve using your money to make it come about?" She folded her arms and gave him a severe look. "It won't be magic if you use your money and connections, Wyatt. I have to be firm on that."

He burst out laughing. "Okay, okay. No money, no connections. I promise. *Now* will you come with me?"

As if she were still considering her decision, she rolled up on her toes, then back on her heels. "How does one dress when going to look for gold and silver?"

"You're perfect just the way you are."

She smiled up at him. "You're a hard man to resist, Wyatt Damaron."

"Apparently not for you."

If he only knew. "I'm going, aren't I?"

He shook his head. "After first making me jump through hoops."

Her brows rose. "If you're not up to it, just tell me."

He reached for her wrist, encircling it with his fingers. "There you go again," he said softly, "challenging me." He looked down at where he held her arm, then back at her. "Be careful, Annie. Be very careful."

She didn't need the warning. Wyatt was a complex man with layers of darkness in him that she knew nothing about. But she had several things going for her. She had faith in herself, her judgment, and her emotional strength. She knew he wouldn't hurt her. And even before the date, she also knew she was going to have a great time.

"Here we are," Wyatt said, spreading a blanket over the sun-warmed grass beside the river.

Annie looked around her in surprise. They were in one of her favorite places, where the river widened and relaxed. In the distance rugged mountains rose to touch the sky. It was nature at its finest and today the sun was showcasing it, flashing glittering bits of light onto the surface of the river, picking out the breaks and the whitecaps of the frolicsome rapids.

Birds gloried in the splendor, flitting from tree to tree, calling out to one another. And across the river squirrels and rabbits, alerted by the turning leaves and shorter days, scurried to store their caches for the coming winter.

"This is our destination?" she asked.

"You don't like it?"

"I *love* it. Elsewhere the river rushes by in a furious hurry, but here, it slows down and plays. And if you listen very carefully, there are times you can actually hear the river laughing."

"Laughing?" Wyatt grinned. "Who else but you could hear a river laugh?"

"You could too if you spent enough time here." She looked up at him. "It's funny you chose this place, but then again I'm not at all surprised. I've always felt that it was kind of magical. I come up here sometimes to be by myself and to think. I've even fallen asleep here a couple of times. I always wake up energized."

He studied her, a slight smile on his face. "It's hard for me to imagine you being anything less than completely energized."

"Everyone gets tired now and then."

"I suppose so."

She chuckled. "You say that like you don't."

He shrugged. "I've never thought about it before. When I get tired, I go to bed. When I wake up, I'm ready to go again."

"Such a practical man," she said dryly.

"Usually. Except when I'm with you."

He'd left his jacket in Scott's truck. The neck of his shirt lay open and his sleeves were rolled up, revealing a strong brown throat and forearms. He looked so rugged and handsome that in that moment he rivaled the glory and magic of his surroundings. Unfortunately she knew he wasn't as permanent.

But that didn't matter. She planned to take advantage of this day and enjoy each golden moment. And in the meantime, he made her feel more alive than she had felt in a long time. It was a heady feeling, headier than the champagne he was uncorking.

"Bertha again?" she said, watching him.

"She's a sweetheart."

She smiled. "She's a tyrant who's obviously succumbed to your charms in a big way." As she dropped down beside him on the blanket, her skirt billowed out around her and settled in a circle of color. She accepted a champagne-filled flute. "All right, I'll bite. What are you with me?"

"Excuse me?"

"You said you're usually a practical man except when you're with me." She was prepared for a flip answer and was surprised when he became thoughtful.

"I haven't gotten it entirely figured out yet. I only know you've tapped something inside me that I'd forgotten all about." Almost absently his hand went to finger the bow that tied her bustier.

"What?" she asked, very aware of his hand so close to her breasts.

He shrugged, releasing the bow. "Maybe it's the part of me that used to love magic."

"You mean the magic tricks you used to play on your family?" She grinned. "Have I awakened a latent wish of yours to become a magician?"

He shook his head. "My explanation about remembering my love of magic is really way too simplistic. It's so much more than that."

She thought for a moment. "There's a magic world of fantasy where, to a certain extent, all children live. It's a world where imagination rules and all things are possible. But when we grow older, everything becomes so complicated that we forget that sometimes it's the simplest things in life that can bring us the greatest joy."

"Thank you," he said quietly. "You perfectly described what I was trying to say."

She nodded. "We all grow up, which is why it's all the more special when we can remember the magic we had inside us when we were young and realize that it still exists in our everyday life. As you have. Last night you used your imagination to set up a situation that, even without the meteor shower, had the potential to be magical. It fulfilled its potential and more."

"All thanks to you," he said, his voice husky, his expression enigmatic. "You challenged me, and you made me remember a lot of things I thought I'd forgotten."

"Then you should be set from now on. Now that you've remembered, you won't forget again." A man like Wyatt wouldn't need anyone for very long, which was fine with her. If she had helped him, he was also helping her, by conjuring up moments of magic that she badly needed.

"Yes," he murmured. "I'm set."

Doing absolutely nothing but talking softly to her, he was mesmerizing. His gaze was spellbinding and perilously easy to fall into. She might be taunting the sorcerer, but he was tempting her with expert control, and she was falling under his spell. Strangely, though, she didn't mind. She was filled with joy when she was with him, and when the joy stopped, she'd pull back and he would leave.

She gave a toss of her head that sent her hair flying over her shoulders. "So where are the mines?"

"Mines?" he said, watching her hair settle around her face and shoulders.

"You said we were going in search of gold and silver."

He stretched his legs out in front of him and returned his attention to her. "What do you see right now, Annie?"

"You." She probably shouldn't have blurted it out as she had, but it was the truth. He filled her vision, and she couldn't look at anything but him. And she realized something else, something startling. She wanted to be filled by him, completely and absolutely. She wanted to make love with him.

She'd wondered last night what she would do when the time came for her to make a definite decision. Well, the time was almost here.

He slowly smiled at her, and her heart beat even faster. "Look around," he said softly, so softly, she had to lean forward to hear him.

She didn't want to look away from him. She wanted to study him, to learn all the lines of his face, the curve of his lips, the texture of his skin, and the shape of his body. God help her, she wanted him with everything that was in her.

"Look around, Annie."

She did, quickly, then returned her gaze to him. "Well?"

"I see a glorious blue sky filled with clouds so full

and white, they might have been painted up there. I see a river that comes pouring out of the mountains, so crystal clear that with the sun on it, it looks like it could be filled with diamonds. I see tall, majestic trees that prove absolutely what Joyce Kilmer wrote, that '. . . only God can make a tree.' "

"You see a lot," he murmured.

"What do you see?"

"I see you and only you. And I want to kiss you more than I want to draw my next breath."

Something inside her shifted, melted, and in the next instant reformed and caught fire. "Well, now," she said, barely breathing, "I can't have you turning purple on me, now can I?"

Slowly, never breaking eye contact with him, she shifted closer to him, positioning her legs over his and stretching them out on either side of his hips until she was settled in the *V* made by his hard thighs.

She cupped his face between her hands and looked deeply into his eyes. "Breathe," she whispered, then leaned forward and pressed her lips to his.

A sound rumbled upward from deep in his chest, a sound of disbelief, amazement, and need. Then he began returning her kiss, lightly at first, following her lead.

A man like Wyatt would be used to having control in all things, she reflected vaguely, but now she was the one in control as she tested the soft fullness of his lips.

The sun was warm on her skin, the breeze gentle as it blew up the ends of her skirt that was already halfway up her thighs. She followed the shape of his lips with her tongue until she'd memorized the outline of them, then slipped her tongue inside the moist warmth of his mouth and met his. This man had to be the all-time best kisser in the history of the world, she thought hazily, wrapping her arms around his neck. Warmth began to filter into her body, taking her over, making her feel instead of think. Yet at the same time, she was incredibly aware of what was happening to her and around her.

There'd never been a more perfect day or a more perfect moment. The sky was a crystalline blue, and nature was at play around them. And inside her, heat had begun to rage, and she felt helpless to stop it. She'd kissed men before, but none of them had ever made her so conscious of the blood rushing through her veins and the heavy, aching feeling in her loins. It was a yearning like none she'd ever known. She increased the pressure of her lips and sent her tongue probing deeper. And she no longer kidded herself that she was in complete control.

His hand slid around her bottom and lifted her until she was sitting on him, and the silk of her panties was pressing down against the rough fabric of his jeans and his hard, bulging sex. A shock went through her, shaking her to her toes, and her bones liquified. Instinctively she began to move against him, trying to get relief from the throbbing need that was growing inside her. Hot thrills of pleasure slammed through her, leaving her shaking. She was close to being lost completely.

Something was telling her she should stop, think,

regain control of herself if only for a moment, but each kiss and each touch he gave her was more electrifying and demanding than the last.

Long ago, she'd learned that tomorrow couldn't be counted on, and that there was only today, only the moment. But at the same time, she tried never to be unthinking or irresponsible. No matter what happened between her and Wyatt next, she felt the instinctive need for a break, even if it was only a short one.

It took every bit of self-control she had left, but she eased away from him until she could no longer feel him against her, and then for good measure, slid back a little more until she was sitting on the ground, though she was still between his thighs. She'd succeeded, she realized, because he had made it easy for her, releasing her as soon as he felt her pull away.

She drew in a deep breath and nervously combed her fingers through her hair. "Congratulations," she said shakily. "I have to say, nothing is more magical than the way you kiss."

Then she looked at him, and in that instant, she saw his steel bared. His face was hard with passion, and his eyes were black as night. Her heart gave a violent thud against her chest.

She'd admitted to herself that she wanted him, but then when the hot reality had hit, she'd pulled back. Before this moment, she hadn't realized that kissing Wyatt for what had been a relatively short amount of time would hurt anything. But she should have known better. In the time it took them to exchange a few sizzling kisses, trees could topple, skies could turn from day to night, heated bodies could lose control—which was what had almost happened.

He expelled a ragged breath, then slowly shook his head. "What am I going to do with you, Annie?"

She ran her tongue over her lips, licking up his taste. "For now—something else. Something else really fast."

He rubbed his face as if he was in pain.

"God, I'm sorry." It was all she knew to say, but it was so inadequate. She'd wanted him a minute ago. She wanted him now. She'd want him ten minutes from now. So why had she pulled away? Because, she suddenly realized, she had felt herself losing control and it was such an unfamiliar feeling to her, it had temporarily frightened her.

He pressed two fingers against her lips. "Don't say that."

He was right, she thought. Words wouldn't help. They'd known each other such a short time, but he had to know as she did that they'd just arrived at a crossroads. One way led to reason and sanity. The other way led to mind-altering, life-altering heat. And right now a feather could push her in the direction of the heat.

"What about the gold and silver?" she said softly. "We got off the subject, but we could try to get back on track."

He rubbed his face again. "Gold and silver?"

"You said we were going in search of gold and silver."

"Oh, right." He looked at her, and she was relieved to see the steel sheathed once more and humor edging into his expression. He nodded his head toward a small pile of shiny new fishing equipment.

"Fishing?" she asked incredulously. "You think fishing is magical?"

"There's fishing and then there's fishing."

"There is?"

"You're not using your imagination, Annie," he chided.

She eased a little farther away from him and tried her best to concentrate. But heat still pounded through her veins, and her body still ached for him. "Okay, then, let's see. There's a couple of fishing poles over there, along with a net. And the fish in the river are wet, scaly, and slippery." He appeared to have already recovered from their kisses, but she had been left feeling fragmented. Mentally trying to pull herself together, she thought for a moment longer. "Yeah, I think that pretty much covers it."

He shook his head. "I have to say I'm disappointed."

She tried to dredge up some semblance of her old spirit. "Aha. So now the shoe's on the other foot and you're challenging *me*. Nice trick, but I never back down from a challenge."

"No? Gee, I wish I'd known that sooner."

Michief played in his eyes, and she felt her heart turn over. Thinking hard, she looked at the fishing equipment and the river. "River. Fish. Hooks, lines, and lures. Okay, okay—something about hooking me." He'd already done that, but she wasn't worried. Many a fish freed itself and swam away. "But where does the gold and silver come in?"

He took her gesturing hand in his. "What's in the river, Annie?"

"Fish."

"What kind of fish?"

She knew she wasn't getting what he wanted her to get, but Lord, it was hard to think rationally when she could still taste his lips on hers and her entire body still throbbed with desire for him. "I gather slippery fish is not the answer?"

"You gather right."

Exasperated at herself for being so slow, she exhaled a long breath. "There are salmon and steelhead trout in the river. Even sitting where we are we can see flashes of them."

He nodded. "That's right. Flashes."

She looked at him quizzically. "So?"

"So what color are they?"

"The salmon are pink. . . ." Light began to dawn. "Well, when the sunlight flashes on their scales they actually look gold. And the trout are silver. Is that it?"

He pulled her back to him until she was close enough that he could lean forward to put his mouth to her ear and whisper,

> "Come live with me, and be my love,
> And we will some new pleasures prove
> Of golden sands, and crystal brooks,
> With silken lines, and silver hooks."

"Oh, Wyatt, how perfect. *John Donne's 'The Bait.'* Gold and silver, crystal and silk—it's all here."

"Donne was the chief sorcerer of all time," he said,

his voice husky with emotion. "His way with words was pure magic."

"You're right," she said, captivated. "But I had no idea you'd know it."

"I learned the poem years ago," he murmured, "and you brought it back to me."

She wanted to ask how, but she didn't. In her mind, "The Bait" was one of the most erotic and beautiful poems ever written. And the importance didn't lie in how or why Wyatt had chosen to recite it to her, but the mere fact that he had.

Wyatt, who was the quintessential man for the twenty-first century, and who lived very much in the present, had conjured up magic by uttering the words of a long-ago metaphysical poet who saw the supernatural in the natural. She was completely enchanted.

Wyatt moved her in his arms and pressed his mouth to her other ear.

> "There will the river whispering run
> Warmed by thy eyes, more than the sun.
> And there th' enamored fish will stay,
> Begging themselves they may betray."

They were getting into dangerous territory, she thought, her pulse racing with excitement. The poet's meaning was enticing and seductive. Donne was talking about women as having the eyes of love and men as the fish, seduced and entranced by a woman's beautiful bait, swimming as sperm into her body.

Wyatt continued, holding her to him, his mouth against her ear.

"When thou wilt swim in that live bath,
Each fish, which every channel hath,
Will amorously to thee swim,
Gladder to catch thee, than thou him."

Her heart gave a thud against her chest that she was sure Wyatt felt. The poet's meaning couldn't have been more sexual or seductive, and Wyatt knew it. The poet's words were begging his lady love to be allowed to enter her body to share the pleasures of love with her.

Without realizing what she was doing, and as if by his command, she moved until she was once again against the hard, throbbing ridge of his sex.

Wyatt groaned. She knew he wanted her. But by choosing parts of this poem to recite to her, he'd completely bewitched her and stepped through any remaining defenses she might have had left, like a man of magic slipping through a wall. And he'd done even more than that. He'd also given her this afternoon of wizardry and enchantment that she'd never forget.

"That was beautiful," she whispered, lifting her head from his shoulder.

"You're beautiful," he whispered back. "John Donne should have known you."

Annie gazed deep into Wyatt's eyes and saw a fierce fire and a hard question. She felt the same fire inside herself, and his question was incredibly easy for her to answer.

"Yes," she said.

FIVE

"Yes? Just like that?"

She nodded. "Just like that."

Another woman might play the artful coquette and try to string him along a little while longer in an attempt to get gifts and promises from him. But not Annie. She'd obviously made a decision and saw no reason to dissemble.

From the first he'd been blown away by her. She was absolutely unique, which was why he'd felt so strongly that she should not be changed by their encounter.

But each time she'd teased and challenged him, each time she'd laughed and returned his kisses, his desire for her had grown. Still he'd held back and denied himself—something he wasn't used to. Within the responsible parameters that he practiced, he rarely thought twice before satisfying any need he might have, physical or otherwise.

But with Annie everything had been different. And

denying himself the pleasure of her had taken a heavy physical toll. He'd spent hours hard and hurting, his body aching with the need for release. He'd lost sleep thinking about what it would be like to be inside her.

He'd always prided himself on his control and so he'd taken great care not to let her know the full extent of his desire for her. But the frustration of wanting her had eaten away at him until he felt there was nothing left of him but nerves and need.

He'd actually thought about flying home. He had several women friends who were always more than happy to oblige him in bed. But he'd been stopped by the knowledge that the true release he needed could only come from Annie. And that knowledge had badly shaken him.

The kind of desire he had for her went beyond wanting. Its scope was enormous. It permeated every pore and cell of his body until it had become a part of him. And now, as easily as drawing breath, she'd said yes and all his honorable intentions had fled.

He eased her down onto her back. Intensified by the blue of the sky, her eyes were a deeper shade than usual, almost a sapphire color, and her hair was spread around her head in a shining, golden arc. Her skin smelled of flowers, and all at once he was overcome by the intensity of his desire for her.

His hands were shaking. He was nervous, he realized. The thought stunned him. He couldn't remember the last time he had been nervous about anything or anyone. But then this was Annie, lying on a blanket in a meadow, waiting for him to make love to her. . . .

She smiled and lifted her hand to caress one side of his face. "You're thinking too much again," she whispered. "It's going to be all right. In fact, it's going to be fabulous."

He took her hand and kissed its palm, and his nervousness fled. No matter what else happened in his life from this point onward, on this day, on this afternoon, in this meadow, he was meant to make love to Annie.

He reached for the lavender satin bow that laced her bodice and pulled at the ribbon, until he could spread the top apart.

And he drew in a sharp breath. Up until now, he'd been a perfect gentleman with her, not even touching her breasts, but now he saw them—round, firm, with delectable pink nipples that were stiff and constricted. Before his heart could beat again, his head was bending toward one. He lathed his tongue around the nipple, then drew it into his mouth and suckled, so hungry for her, he wasn't sure he'd be able to stop.

Her hands closed in his hair. "Wyatt," she murmured, as if she were melting, and her tone melted *him*.

From the moment he'd met her, he'd treated her with gentleness, but the white-hot passion that was coiling tighter and tighter in his gut wasn't compatible with gentleness. What he was feeling was raw and primitive, hot and hungry.

Annie deserved to be made love to with care and finesse and by someone whose intentions toward her went beyond the physical. She deserved all of that and more, but *he* was the one who was about to make love to her and he wasn't going to be able to do any of those things.

Blood thundered through his veins and pounded in his ears. He pushed her skirt up around her waist, then closed his hand around the top of her panties and pulled them off her. Just as hastily he undressed and sheathed himself with protection, then positioned himself between her thighs.

He should say something to her, he thought through a haze. Caress her to make sure she was ready. But she was looking up at him, meeting his gaze, fearless and beautiful, and he couldn't wait any longer.

He pulled back his hips and thrust with all his force into her, and miracle of miracles, she received him with a soft moan of satisfaction. A fiery, exquisite sensation shot through him, nearly stopping his heart. He trembled at its force and intensity. Then he did something he'd never done before, something he wouldn't have thought he *could* do. He stilled, closed his eyes, and gave himself over to the incredible, shimmering heat, as it infused every part of his being.

Seconds later, he felt her arch up to him, her hands moving restlessly over his back. "You feel wonderful inside me," she whispered.

With a deep groan, he bent his head to kiss her lips, and at the same time drove into her hard and fast. His reaction to her was primitive.

He'd always been skilled and controlled in lovemaking, but not with Annie. With Annie he didn't have a chance. He was lost and totally overpowered by her—by her soft, willing body beneath his, by her sweet fragrance that enveloped him, by the longing in her voice that drove him on.

She wrapped her long, silken legs around his hips and lifted her pelvis, meeting him, taking him even deeper into her with a rhythm that exactly matched his. Her body was strong, and she responded to his every movement. She seemed to know what he was going to do before he did. It was a melding of their flesh, their minds, and their souls.

As was Annie's way she held back nothing, and because of it, there was a full-blown passion and a hot, naked desire that was joining them together. Wyatt tried to fight his own response, tried to make the heat and ecstasy last for her, but the undulation and rolling of her hips was making that impossible.

She was a seductress with feminine ways as old as time, yet he felt as if everything with her was a first. He was completely wrapped up with her, by her. He groaned again as an uncontrollable tension began to build in him. He was starving for air, for her, for release.

But once again Annie anticipated and was in perfect synchronization with him. She clutched his shoulders, stiffened, and cried out his name as she began the swift, hot, powerful ascent to her climax, and in the same moment an unbearable pleasure exploded in him. He held her tight and rocked against her as his body convulsed and a sweet madness overtook him.

Minutes or hours might have passed, he wasn't sure. He felt her beneath him, her skin damp with sweat as his was, her muscles trembling as his were, her breathing uneven and rapid as his was. Moving slowly, he rolled off her, and clasped her hand firmly in his.

His chest heaved as he fought for breath, but the breeze blew across his naked body, cooling his skin and slowly righting the world around him, the world that had spun so wildly out of control as he had made love to Annie.

He turned his head to look at her. Her eyes were closed, her breasts were rising and falling rapidly as she too tried to gulp down air. Her skin was flushed, and the only piece of clothing she still wore was her skirt bunched around her waist. He couldn't remember ever feeling so satisfied, and yet being left wanting much, much more.

He waited until his breathing returned to normal, then stripped the skirt from her. Irregardless of what happened next between them, he wanted her completely naked beside him.

Without saying a word, she turned toward him. He slid his arm beneath her and pulled her against him so that her head was resting on his shoulder. As naturally as if she'd done it a hundred times before, she looped one leg over his and placed her hand on his chest.

He'd vowed not to touch her, not to change her, but that vow had vanished on a wellspring of hot desire and now he'd done much more than touch her. He couldn't regret what had just happened, and lying there with her, her naked body pressed against his, their only covering the sky above them, he knew he didn't have to worry about her.

Without a doubt, he now understood that she was

still the same untouched, unaffected, lovely woman she'd always been, and that instead of her being changed, *he* had been. He didn't know how or to what extent yet, but he knew he would never be the same again.

The good-night kiss Wyatt had given her at her door had almost undone her, Annie mused, standing at her kitchen counter, waiting for her tea to brew. More than anything, she'd wanted to pull him into the house and ask him to stay the night with her, but she'd resisted. Wyatt certainly hadn't wanted to go, but in the end, he had.

It had been a wondrous afternoon with a miraculous man, and she didn't regret for a minute what had happened between them. After they'd made love the first time, they'd made love again, and each time, they'd connected physically and emotionally in an utterly amazing way. Making love to him had been the ultimate magic.

But after all the magic that had passed between them, after all the kisses and lovemaking, she now needed some time to herself. Quite simply he'd overwhelmed her and she needed time alone to regain her balance and perspective.

She poured the steaming tea into a cup and took it into the living room. She'd already checked that there'd been nothing rearranged or added. Now she was more sure than ever that the pranks had a direct correlation to the faire. Relaxed, she sank into the corner of her couch, and sipping her tea, she continued trying to sort through her thoughts about Wyatt.

He'd come to the area on vacation to relax and enjoy himself, and she'd been ready to help him. But she'd honestly never thought it would go as far as it had. What had happened in the meadow between them might be the norm for him, but it certainly wasn't for her.

Thankfully, for all the extraordinary things that had happened, there were two things that had remained constant from the first: the fact that he wouldn't be staying in the area long, and the fact that she wouldn't fall in love with him. Those two things would be her saving grace.

Because making love to Wyatt had shaken her to her core, and if she were any other woman, she'd have been head over heels in love by now.

Fortunately love wasn't involved between them—only physical passion. And passion, though hard to handle in the moment, always faded. And when it was all over, she'd have the memories of the time they'd spent together, and they would be glorious memories indeed.

She finished her tea, washed the cup in the kitchen sink, then headed for her bedroom. She raised the windows, allowing the cool breeze in. She could smell rain in the air. It would be a good night for sleeping, she thought, then smiled. It would be an even better night for making love. . . .

For a moment she toyed with the idea of driving over to the cabin and knocking on the door. The temptation was strong, but she was tired, she realized. Plus, she could feel the beginnings of a headache starting behind her eyes. A good night's sleep would have her feeling much better tomorrow.

She pulled back the bedcovers and froze. The sightless eyes of a dead bird stared back at her, its feathers a grotesque black shape against her white sheets.

Slowly she backed away from the bed, a sob rising in her throat. Why was this happening to her? What did it all mean?

A cry escaped her, and bile began to rise in her throat. She picked up the phone and dialed the number of the sheriff.

The sheriff, a big, husky man with a balding head, had come and gone. To give him his due, he had arrived within ten minutes of her call. He had seemed genuinely sympathetic and had had her go through everything that had been happening, right from the start.

She'd wrapped her arms around her waist, trying to hold herself together, and had tried to answer his questions, but with her headache steadily increasing, she'd had a hard time concentrating.

When he'd asked the inevitable "Do you have any enemies, Ms. Logan?" she'd said no, then realized she'd just lied to him.

But like an ostrich with its head firmly stuck in the sand, she still wasn't ready to face what that would mean. She clung to the fact that the style was still wrong—at least that's what she fervently wanted to believe. Unless . . .

Unless they had decided to go about their business in a different way in an effort to camouflage their identity. The thought made her go cold. Because if that was the case, she'd just played right into their hands by notifying the sheriff of what he must think of as small, innocuous events.

She was still thinking about that when he'd asked, "Can you think of any reason why someone would want to scare you?" She'd automatically said no, then seconds later remembered Dennis. If he *was* trying to scare her into needing him, then he was stepping up his efforts and getting more serious about it.

But the alternative was so frightening for her, she prayed the culprit was Dennis. She could handle him.

The sheriff eventually left, promising to drive by her house on a more regular basis, and to return the next day with his fingerprinting kit. He'd also disposed of the dead bird for her. She'd been very grateful.

After he left, she'd immediately gone to the medicine cabinet and downed some aspirin, then turned her attention to the bed. She'd stripped the sheets, thrown them in the washing machine, poured bleach and soap in, and turned it on. She didn't know if she could ever bring herself to sleep on them again, but whatever she did with them, at least they'd be clean and disinfected.

Unfortunately the burst of activity had worsened her headache. With a hand to her pounding head, she'd looked around her, and was certain that she couldn't stay alone in her house that night.

She pulled her car to a stop in front of the cabin and turned off the motor. Lights were on inside, and smoke curled from the chimney. She was afraid and hurting and past thought. All she knew was that Wyatt was inside and she desperately needed his magic to make her pain and fear go away.

She stumbled out of the car and somehow was able to climb the stairs to the door. She didn't know if she knocked or not, but the door opened and Wyatt was standing there. He smiled when he saw her, then as his gaze raked over her, he slowly paled. The next thing she knew, she was falling into his arms.

"Annie, my God, what's happened?"

"I hurt . . . my head." It was all she could manage to say.

He carried her to the couch and carefully laid her down amid a myriad of soft pillows. "What happened? Did you knock your head against something? Did you fall and hit your head?"

There was very little light in the cabin, but even the smallest amount against her eyes was intolerable. She shut them. "No. Headache."

"How long have you had it?"

"A couple of hours."

"Have you taken anything for it?"

"Aspirin."

"I'll be right back."

She didn't want him to leave her, but she couldn't get one more word out. She wasn't used to pain. She was rarely sick, and she *never* had headaches. Except lately. Stress was the culprit, of course.

She'd tried her best to keep calm and find a reasonable explanation for the strange occurrences in her home. But finding the dead bird in her bed tonight had done her in. She was no longer dealing with silly pranks. The bird had clearly been an ominous sign.

The nearby fire was doing a good job of warming her and soothing away the shivers that had been racking her body since she'd first seen the bird. The pain in her head hadn't yet abated, but at least her fear was easing. On some level, just being with Wyatt was making her feel better. She heard him return to the room and felt his weight as he sank down beside her on the sofa.

"I have something I want you to take," he said quietly.

"What?"

"Something stronger than the aspirin, but don't worry, it won't hurt you."

She wasn't worried. When the cabin door had opened and Wyatt had caught her in his strong arms, she'd stopped worrying. Besides, at this point she'd take anything if it would just stop her pain. He slipped his arm beneath her shoulders and carefully raised her so that she could take the pill and drink the water he offered. As soon as she was through he eased her back down among the pillows and set the glass of water aside.

"God, Annie, you're white as a sheet. I'm giving that pill thirty minutes to work, but if you're not better by then, I'm calling a doctor."

"No." Now that she was there with him, she didn't want to move for a long, long time.

"I can't believe you drove in this much pain. You

should have called me, and I would have come right over."

He was speaking softly, but she could still hear the frustration in his voice. She started to tell him she didn't have his phone number, but then she remembered that he had given it to her yesterday when he came to her shop. At any rate, she'd needed to get away from her house and the image of that dead bird. . . .

Wyatt gently pressed a cool cloth against her forehead, and the pressure felt wonderful, as if his hand on the cloth was keeping the pain contained. And why not—he was magic, wasn't he? After a minute he stripped the cloth away. She wrinkled her forehead and made a sound of protest.

"Shhh," he murmured, and quickly replaced it with a cooler one.

Keeping her eyes closed, she stopped fighting the pain and relaxed. Wyatt talked quietly to her, though it was too much effort for her to keep up with what he was saying. Occasionally he would shift beside her or get up and leave, but she came to know that he would always come back. And with him he brought a warm blanket, a glass of ice water, another moist cloth. Eventually she drifted off to sleep.

Wyatt watched her as he dipped the cloth into the cool water, wrung it out, and returned it to her forehead. She was sleeping, which had to mean the intensity of the headache had lessened. Didn't it?

When she'd first arrived, his first impulse had been to bundle her into the car and rush her to the nearest hospital, but it was obvious that any more movement than she'd already experienced would be excruciating to her. He'd decided to see what he could do first, and thank goodness he'd remembered Scott's telling him he kept a well-stocked medicine cabinet in case of accidents. Sure enough he'd found a prescription painkiller, and it seemed as if it had finally kicked in. Thank God. Her pain had been hard for him to bear.

She still looked pale, he thought. And very, very frail. Had he done the right thing in not taking her to the hospital? He wasn't sure. But if she turned worse in any way, he could always summon help with his cell phone.

Reason told him that she didn't have chronic headaches. She'd come to him for help and comfort, which meant she wasn't used to handling headaches of that magnitude by herself.

So what could have caused it? She'd been fine when he'd said good night to her at her door.

He sighed. In the short time he'd known her, she'd become the center of his thoughts and the sole reason he'd stayed in the area, since he didn't know when or even if Scott would ever show up. Yet he knew relatively little about her.

Before she'd arrived, he'd been thinking about her and the way she had of never doing anything by halves. During the afternoon, she would turn her head to look at him or raise her hand to gesture and sensuality would ooze from her pores and cause heat to flow into his. When she kissed him, she did so with body and soul, and each time his gut would twist, knot, and hurt with desire. Then she would smile and laugh, and his heart would swell.

There was no part of him she didn't affect.

When he'd awoken this morning, thinking of Annie, the John Donne poem had come into his head. He hadn't thought of the poem in years, but once he remembered it, he'd thought up the twist of showing her gold and silver that had no intrinsic monetary value.

He hadn't consciously set out to seduce her. It was only when he'd first begun to recite the poem that the meaning of the words had come back to him. As he'd continued, the fierceness with which he'd wanted her had grown and thoughts of protecting her from himself had fled.

Looking back, it had been extremely egocentric of him to think that his lovemaking would be powerful enough to change her. He should have known that no one would be able to change the unique being that was Annie.

His cell phone rang in the bedroom. He lightly caressed her cheek, assuring himself that she was resting comfortably, then rose and went to answer the phone.

"Hey, Wyatt, how's the fishing?"

He smiled at the sound of his cousin Sinclair's voice. "I wouldn't have a clue. So far I haven't done any. Scott hasn't been around since I got here."

"That's a shame. I know how much you were looking forward to the fishing."

He grinned. "Well, I could have given it a go by myself, but I decided to wait for Scott."

"Any idea when he'll be back?"

"Not a clue."

"Well, good. Then I don't feel so bad interrupting your vacation, since it doesn't sound like you've had much of one anyway."

Wyatt glanced around the bedroom door at Annie. She was still sleeping. He eased the door closed, but didn't let the lock catch. "What's up?"

"It's our communication merger. We've got a watchdog group yapping at our heels, and they're becoming a real pain in the ass."

"Exactly how much of a pain?"

"They've been running newspaper ads for some time now, but just this past week they've started TV ads."

"Are they saying anything libelous?"

"No, they're being very careful. But what's annoying is that the concerns they're voicing in their ads are baseless. It's all speculation, but the general public doesn't know that."

"We can tell them."

"We're working up some ads now, though I don't know if it'll do any good. It might just sound defensive."

"Then we're going to have to deal with the watchdog group and convince them that what we want to do will be good for all concerned. Then get them to back off and print a retraction."

"You're right. That's why I need you back here."

Wyatt groaned, and glanced in the direction of the living room.

"I'm sorry," Sin went on, "but the rest of us are tied

up. Gus White is the person who's been dealing with the group for us up to now."

"He's one of the best."

"I know he is, but he's not a Damaron, and frankly I don't think anyone else is going to make an impression on these people. If they see that a Damaron has made the effort to come before them and address their concerns, then they'll sit up and listen and hopefully be convinced that we really do care and that we intend to do everything absolutely right. So, is coming back a problem for you?"

Wyatt considered his cousin's question, and the very fact that he had to take the time to consider the question astonished him. Of course he was going. His family needed him.

"Wyatt?"

"I'll be there, Sin. If everything is okay here, I'll fly out first thing in the morning."

"What do you mean if everything is okay there?"

His lips twisted wryly. Sin caught everything. "There's something going on here that I want to make sure is okay before I leave. I'll explain when I see you tomorrow. In the meantime, have a jet here for me at six-thirty A.M. PST."

"Will do."

"Also, have all pertinent documents and records on this issue on board the plane. I'll have a five-hour commute back to New York to study them."

"Anything else?"

"Contact all parties involved in the watchdog group

and advise them that I will be holding a meeting at Damaron Tower tomorrow evening at seven P.M. EST."

"You sure you don't want more time? It's a pretty complicated issue."

He had no idea why he felt the urgency to tackle this problem so quickly, but he did. "I'll have enough time, and if nothing else, the meeting will be a good start. I already know some things about it from our last quarterly meeting. Have my assistants standing by all day long tomorrow. Tell them I'll be calling them from the plane. Also notify Gus White. Tell him I want him at the meeting too. Oh, and one last thing. Make sure there's a helicopter waiting for me at the airport to fly me to the Tower. I don't want any lost time."

"That's automatic for any of us, you know that," Sin said, concern creeping into his voice. "What's going on?"

Wyatt paused. "I have a lot on my mind right now. I've met someone—"

Relief filled Sin's chuckle. "Say no more. I understand completely. We'll talk tomorrow."

"Right. See you then." Wyatt closed his cell phone and stared down at it. He didn't want to go. Dammit, *he didn't want to go*. And knowing that Annie was the reason he didn't want to go made no sense to him at all.

True, since he'd known her, she'd managed to completely engross him. But with him and his cousins, their family always came first. *Always*. No questions, no hesitation. He supposed he was simply concerned for her health, but that problem was easily solved. If she still wasn't feeling well in the morning, he'd take her to the hospital before he left.

"Wyatt?"

He turned around to see Annie swaying in front of him. "What are you doing up?"

Her hand went to her head. "I'm feeling better."

"Yeah, you look like it." Her face was white to the lips, except for violet smudges in the delicate skin beneath her eyes. He took her hand and led her back to the couch. "Sit down and don't move. If you need something, tell me."

She touched her head again. "My headache is better."

"Good, but you've still got that pain medicine in you."

"I do feel a little woozy," she said.

"Did the sound of the phone ringing wake you up?"

"No." Her brow furrowed over his question. "I think I woke up because I sensed you weren't sitting beside me any longer."

Something moved in him. If Sin knew about Annie's way with words, he'd send *her* to talk to the watchdog group. He knelt in front of her. "You said your headache is better, but is there any pain left?"

She held up her hand close to her head and gestured. "Just the silent echo of the pain, you know?"

"No."

"It feels like the pain should be there, but it's not. It's more the memory of the pain." She licked her lips, and he immediately held up the water glass to her lips.

She took several sips, then leaned back. "That was some pill you gave me."

"Percodan—Scott keeps some on hand in case of emergencies. I'm glad it worked."

"It did. Wyatt," she said slowly, "I can't tell you how sorry I am to have showed up on your doorstep like I did this evening."

"There's nothing to apologize for. You did the right thing." He rose from his kneeling position and took a seat beside her on the couch.

"No, I intruded on your evening. I'm very embarrassed."

"Don't be." He enfolded her hands with his. "You shouldn't have been home alone in that much pain, Annie. Absolutely no way." He gazed at her worriedly. "Do you have that kind of headache often?"

"I've *never* had that kind of headache."

"So why do you think you got it?"

She hesitated. "I don't know."

He shrugged. "Well, I don't suppose it matters, as long as you don't get another one." He stood up. "I'm going to fix you something to eat."

She put her hand over her stomach. "I'm not sure I could keep anything down."

"I'll make it light. Maybe a consommé. Scott has all sorts of canned goods stocked away in the kitchen. I'm sure there's some broth."

Maybe he was right, she thought as he disappeared into the kitchen. With the pain gone, maybe a bit of food would help her get over this weak feeling more quickly.

She leaned her head against a cushion and closed her eyes, and before she knew it, Wyatt was back, carrying a tray. "Consommé and crackers," he said, setting it on the coffee table. "Plus a few pieces of cheese. Eat what looks good to you and leave the rest."

She lifted a spoonful of broth to her mouth and discovered that even that small effort was too much for her. "It's the pill," he murmured, taking the spoon and carefully feeding her. "It's making you feel woozy. Plus it's after midnight and normally you're probably asleep by now anyway."

"Normally," she agreed, and accepted another spoonful of soup. She reached for a cracker and slowly munched on it. "I'm being a lot of trouble."

He smiled. "I thought I'd wait until you're feeling better to give you my bill."

"I'm serious, Wyatt."

"You shouldn't be." He spooned more soup into her.

When she'd arrived, she'd been in so much pain, she had barely seen him. But now she saw he was still wearing the jeans he'd had on earlier in the day and a different shirt that hung loose and open. He must have grabbed it and shrugged it on when he'd heard her knock at the door. She felt incredibly foolish and embarrassed at having him see her so weak. The afternoon had been so perfect, but the evening had quickly turned into a nightmare for her. She hated it that she'd ruined his evening too. When he offered her another spoonful of soup, she held up her hand. "No more."

"All right." He picked up the tray and took it into

the kitchen, and when he returned she was on her feet. "What do you want? Just tell me and I'll get it for you."

"Thank you, but I'm much better now and I can get whatever I need." She looked around her and saw several closed doors. "Which way is the bathroom?"

He pointed. "Through the bedroom."

She nodded. "I'll be back in a few minutes."

"Annie, are you sure—?"

"I can walk by myself, Wyatt, but if you hear me fall, you have my permission to come and rescue me. Okay?"

"Okay," he said, but didn't look happy about it.

Walking the short distance to the bathroom wasn't as easy as she'd thought it would be. She felt dizzy and weaker than she would have liked to admit.

When she returned to the living area, she found Wyatt pacing. "You're staying here tonight," he said, his expression set.

She didn't even think about arguing. She didn't want to be by herself, nor did she want to go home to the stripped bed and the possibility of another prank. She'd be better able to face the whole thing in the morning when the pill was out of her system and the sun was up and shining into all corners of her house. But not tonight. She pointed toward the couch. "I'll sleep here."

"You'll sleep on the bed," he said, turning her and guiding her into the room she'd just passed through.

"But—"

"You're going to sleep with me tonight in Scott's

extra bedroom. This way if you get sick during the night, I'll be right beside you."

She didn't have the energy to argue with him. Besides he was making perfect sense. And after the hours they'd spent that afternoon, making love, what was the point of trying to be modest?

Tomorrow, she told herself. If she could just hold herself together until tomorrow, she'd see the events of tonight in a better light. At least she hoped she would.

SIX

Wyatt leaned his chair back on two legs and propped his feet on top of the porch railing, a cup of coffee in his hand. He loved the early-morning hours. The minute the first sun rays of the day peeked over the horizon, his eyes automatically opened and his adrenaline started pumping. He always felt an electricity in the air for the exciting promise of the new day ahead.

But today there was another reason he was up early. *Annie.*

All night he'd cradled her in his arms, though he doubted if she'd been aware of it. She'd slept so soundly, so quietly, there'd been times he wondered if she was still alive. Those were the times when he'd lower his head to her breast and lay his ear over her heart to reassure himself that she was indeed still breathing. Fighting the pain of her headache had worn her out. When the Percodan had finally kicked in and given her relief, she had gone right to sleep.

Sipping at his coffee, he tried to figure out what could have brought on such a vicious headache in the first place. She'd told him she'd never had that kind of headache before, but now that she'd had one, there were no guarantees that she wouldn't have another. Medical conditions could develop overnight.

He was overdue to leave for New York, but he was waiting for her to wake up so that he could see for himself how she was doing. After he left, if she had another headache as severe as the one she'd had last night, he wouldn't be here for her. *Who would take care of her then?* The question was another reason he hadn't slept much the night before.

His lips formed a firm line. As soon as she woke up he was going to tell her to make a doctor's appointment for this afternoon and get a thorough checkup.

He stopped himself midthought. On second thought, the idea would go over much better if he *suggested* the idea to her rather than *told* her. He smiled to himself.

It wasn't that she was obstinate. She was just an extremely independent young woman. She ran her own business and, judging by what he'd seen, quite successfully too. She lived alone and seemed to like it—otherwise she would have changed her living arrangements long before now. She had the ability to make a man come undone simply by smiling at him, but by her own words, she had no plans to ever permanently attach herself to a man and fall in love. She was obviously very happy with her life.

But last night when she'd been in pain, she'd come to him.

A shiny red sports car wheeled into the drive, and amid a spray of gravel came to a stop. The driver-side door opened, and a tall, blond-haired man got out of the car. Dark sunglasses concealed his expression as he turned his head to stare up at the house and Wyatt.

The front chair legs hit the floor, and Wyatt rose. Setting his coffee cup on the porch railing, he ambled down to greet the man.

"One of these days," Wyatt said with a broad grin, "I'm going to have to teach you how to read a calendar. You'll be amazed at how useful it can be in keeping your life straight—you know, like *where* you're supposed to be and *when*."

"Unfortunately," Scott drawled, pushing his sunglasses to the top of his head, "not even the most advanced computer in the world could keep my life straight."

With a big laugh, Wyatt threw his arm around Scott, and the two men gave each other a series of hearty pats on their backs.

"I see you're still as ugly as ever," Scott said, pulling back, "but *damn*, it's good to see you."

Wyatt grinned again. "I was just thinking the same thing about you."

Scott leaned against the car and eyed his friend speculatively. "I saw one of those snazzy Damaron jets of yours sitting out at the airport." He paused. "All the systems were on. I don't suppose that means you've just gotten here."

"Unfortunately, it means I'm about to leave." Wyatt shot back the cuff of his shirt and looked at his watch. "As a matter of fact, I should have been out of here a couple of hours ago."

Scott shook his head. "I'm sorry I couldn't get here on time, but something came up, and I just couldn't refuse to go."

Wyatt nodded. "I understand. Some things have to come first."

Scott was what some might call an independent contractor. But he was a very *special* contractor. His contracts nearly always came from a top secret section of the government and involved travel around the world to the various hot spots of the moment. Scott rarely talked about his work and then only in the most general of terms, but from what Wyatt had been able to surmise, Scott had spent a lot of his time in the last few years in the Middle East.

"However," Wyatt added jokingly, "just because I understand doesn't get you off the hook entirely. If I were you, I'd sleep with the light on for a while."

Scott chuckled. "You want retribution, huh?"

"Maybe. Maybe not. The not knowing will be hell for you."

"Hey, if it makes you feel any better, I hated every minute I couldn't be here. I kept thinking about all the good fishing I was missing."

Wyatt grinned. "I'll forgive you only if there was torture involved for you."

Scott grimaced. "There very nearly was."

And just like that, all joking stopped. Wyatt had seen

Scott six months before in New York. Looking at him now, though, he realized that there were new lines in Scott's face and more gray at his temples. "Bad, huh?"

"Some uninvited guests showed up at our party and threw the whole damn thing off." He folded his arms across his chest. "By the way, a good friend of your family was along on this one."

"David?"

"Yep, and he just about single-handedly saved the situation."

"He's okay?"

"He's fine. He ran into a bullet or two, but one was a flesh wound and the other went straight through his shoulder without hitting anything." Scott casually gestured to the spots on his own body.

"Aunt Abigail will be relieved."

"You think he'll tell her?"

Wyatt chuckled. "Probably not. Aunt Abigail can get anything out of anyone, but David is her godson, her *beloved* godson, who in her opinion can do no wrong. David can wind her around his little finger. It's a joy to watch." He paused. "Sounds like David was lucky."

"Luck didn't have a damn thing to do with it. Very few people in our business are as good as David is."

"Better than you?" Wyatt said, deliberately trying to lighten things up again. It worked.

Scott's eyes narrowed on Wyatt. "Get a grip, Damaron. *No* one is better than I am." Wyatt laughed, and Scott leaned into the car and pulled out a bag. "Have you gotten any fishing in?"

"No, but I have gotten to see a lot of the area." He needed to tell Scott about Annie, and quickly, since she happened to be sleeping in one of Scott's beds. He wished he didn't have to, though. He would have liked to keep their relationship between the two of them. He wasn't sure why, but maybe he feared that magic, when exposed to the light of reality, would disintegrate. But it was a ridiculous thought, since he was about to leave and chances were good he'd never see her again.

Scott rubbed his hand over his face. "Man, I hate that our vacation got screwed up. I've been looking forward to this for months."

"I know. I have too. But you'll be happy to know that my time here has accomplished one thing. I'm finally convinced the area is as beautiful as you've always said it was." He'd also met Annie, an amazing woman who had discovered magic in him.

Scott's expression lightened. "It's great, isn't it? I'm telling you, I would have gone crazy a long time ago if I didn't have this place to come home to."

"I can see it. Listen, I'm flying back to New York to handle a problem we're having. As soon as I get it settled, I'll get in touch with you and we can plan another vacation. Maybe as soon as the end of next week."

What he'd just said made no sense, Wyatt realized. Seconds ago, he'd decided he'd probably never see Annie again and now he was planning to come back next week? Perhaps it was just as well he was leaving. Obviously he needed space to clear his mind so that he could view the time he'd spent with Annie more logically and rationally.

Scott was shaking his head. "End of next week?" He smiled somewhat sheepishly. "I'm afraid I *also* have a jet waiting at the airport. Tomorrow, I'm meeting up with David again in Paris. When the uninvited guests showed up at the party and then David was wounded, we decided it was best to withdraw, get his wounds seen to, and develop a new plan. As you might imagine, we're both anxious to get our loose ends tied up, but I have no idea how long it's going to take."

Wyatt looked at him with a frown. "So this is just a quick visit?"

"*Really* quick. I'll be flying out again this afternoon. David checked into a plush hotel in Paris to recuperate for a few days. Normally I would have checked in there with him. We could have worked on our plans and at the same time had a little R and R."

"So why didn't you?"

"I knew you were here and I wanted to see you, even if it was only for a few hours. David and I will still have time to plan our next move if I leave this afternoon."

Wyatt shook his head. "You should have stayed in Paris with David."

Scott's mouth widened into a big grin. "Oh, if it had *only* been you, I would have, no question." His grin slid away. "But this way I also have a few hours to fill up my lungs with this great mountain air and have a nice long walk in the woods. I go into withdrawal if I can't do that every so often. It keeps me grounded." The grin reappeared, along with his tongue firmly placed in his cheek. "Seeing you was a by-product really."

The two men laughed, and Scott started off toward

the house. "Come on, Damaron. You can afford ten more minutes out of your schedule to tell me what you've seen and done since you've been here."

Wyatt fell into step beside him. "Scott, there's something I need to—" He saw Annie's car parked by the side of the house. Damn. He'd forgotten about it.

Scott saw it at the same time. "Hey, you know, that car looks just like the car a friend of mine drives. *Annie!*"

Wyatt looked up and saw Annie strolling out onto the porch. At the sight of her, he felt his heart pick up a beat. Despite her ordeal of the night before, she looked fresh and lovely, with her hair combed straight and shining around her shoulders, and a smile on her face for Scott. She was dressed in the same skirt and top she'd had on all yesterday and miraculously it didn't seem to be too wrinkled. Best of all, there was no sign of the pain that had held her in its grip during the night.

"Annie, how great to see you, but what are you—?" Suddenly Scott looked at Wyatt, then back at her. "Ah." He nodded. "Sorry. Normally I'm much quicker. I must be more tired than I think I am. Never mind. I see you've met Wyatt."

Without the least sign of embarrassment at the situation, Annie sauntered down the stairs to the two men. "Yes," she said, leaning forward to kiss Scott on his cheek. "We met the night Wyatt arrived, and we've been having a lot of fun ever since."

Scott threw his arm around Wyatt's shoulder. "If I've said it once, I've said it a million times—Wyatt's fun."

She smiled. "Be nice, Scott."

Wyatt frowned. The way she'd said they'd been having fun made it seem as if they'd been nothing more than casual friends. But then what was wrong with that? He certainly didn't want her to tell Scott about everything they'd shared. Plus, he supposed that, strictly speaking, they really were nothing more than friends. No promises had been made or asked for. Still, a hard knot formed in his stomach. "How are you feeling, Annie?"

"Fine, thank you." She turned to Scott to explain. "Poor Wyatt. I had the mother of all headaches last night, and I showed up on his doorstep, barely able to see. Fortunately he had the presence of mind to give me one of your pain pills. Knocked the headache right out."

Scott's lips twisted wryly. "And you, too, I would imagine."

"Oh, in a major way." She smiled up at him. "It's wonderful to see you again, and I know Wyatt is happy you're home. Now you two can finally start your vacation."

Scott ran his hand around the back of his neck. "You don't know how I wish that were the case. I've got to be on my way again in a few hours, and Wyatt is leaving even sooner than that."

"Really?" Her tone was as calm as if Scott had told her the sky was blue. Slowly she turned her head and looked at Wyatt. "For some reason I thought you said you'd decided to stay a little longer. I was obviously mistaken."

He would have much preferred to have told her the news in private, but Scott had no way of knowing that. In fact, Scott probably assumed she already knew. "No, you weren't mistaken. I *had* made that decision, but last night while you were sleeping, my cousin Sin called. There's some business I need to handle."

"I see," she said, her smile spread equally between the two men. "Any chance you'll get back this way soon?"

"Probably not." He silently cursed himself. It was what he always said in these kinds of situations when he was saying good-bye to a woman, but this time it disturbed him. He even saw Scott looking at him oddly, as well he should, since minutes ago he'd told Scott he might be able to make it back by the end of next week. He definitely wasn't handling this right.

"Well, at least you managed to have a few days of vacation, which is always nice."

She was smiling at him, just as she'd always done. Except she'd withdrawn. He could feel it as surely as if a cold wind had just blown over him.

She glanced at Scott. "Are you back for a while?"

"Nope. I've got to leave again this afternoon."

"Well, I hope this trip won't be long and that you'll be back soon. Wyatt, thanks for your help last night. Both of you have a safe flight." She raised her hand. "Bye."

"Wait," Scott said. "Wyatt was just going to tell me about all he'd seen since he's been here. Why not stay and contribute?"

Regretfully, she shook her head. "I'd love to, but I

need to go home and change so that I can open the shop. Oh, Wyatt, I almost forgot to say how glad I am we met. I really enjoyed our time together."

She held out her hand to him, and he was so stunned, he took it. But then she pulled her hand back and the contact with her was gone.

They'd never talked about the time when he would leave, and now that he thought about it, he realized it was because of Annie and her incredible gift for living in the present.

He'd had women, when he'd told them he was leaving, throw questions and accusations at him, not to mention priceless porcelains and crystal. He should have known that wouldn't be Annie's style. She was accepting his leaving with dignity and class and without regrets.

"Scott, I'm going to walk her to her car."

"Sure," he said agreeably, but his expression plainly stated he had no intention of letting Wyatt leave for the airport until he had received an explanation. "I'll be inside. I badly need a shower and a cup of coffee and not necessarily in that order. Annie, see you next time."

"Yeah." She suddenly snapped her fingers. "Oh, *hey*, I just remembered something. You better get back here quick. Our Autumn Fest is coming up in a couple of days."

"Damn." Scott smacked his forehead with the heel of his hand.

Annie smiled ruefully at him. "Don't tell me, let me guess."

Scott shook his head. "Sorry, hon. Next year, I promise."

"Yeah, yeah," she teased affectionately. "That's what you say every year."

"And as always, I mean it too."

"And as always you'll be missed."

"Thanks, hon."

She waved to him. "Bye."

Wyatt caught up with her and put his hand on her arm to slow her down. "I owe you an apology."

"An apology?" she asked with puzzlement. "Whatever for?"

"I should have been the one to tell you I'm leaving."

"Why?" she asked in mild surprise. "What difference does it make who told me?"

"Because you should have heard it from me first. It's just that I was trying to let you sleep as long as possible, but then Scott arrived, and he just assumed you knew, and—"

"No problem." She gave a nonchalant shrug. "By the way, the T-shirt you put on me last night? I assumed it was yours and not Scott's, and I threw it in your carry-on bag. Your other suitcase was locked."

"Yeah, it's packed and ready to go."

"I should have guessed."

"I hope you don't mind that I changed you. I just figured you'd rest better if you were out of your skirt and top."

She reached out and patted his arm. "Stop worrying. You did everything right. And I'm sure I did rest better. Thanks again for all your help last night."

They arrived at her car, but his hand beat hers to the door handle, keeping it closed. She looked up at him inquiringly. "Annie, about yesterday afternoon."

"Yesterday afternoon? Yes, it was fun, wasn't it?"

"Fun?"

"And our lovemaking was wonderful, of course," she added quickly as if she feared she'd hurt his feelings. "Really wonderful. You know," she said softly, "I'm very glad I ran into you on that foggy path the night you arrived." She rose up on her tiptoes and gently kissed his cheek. "I really need to go now. I don't want to be late opening the store."

If he would have imagined their parting, it certainly wouldn't have been like this—hurried on her part and uncomfortable and awkward on his. He felt like a clumsy schoolboy, while she . . . Well, the moment she'd heard he was leaving, she had mentally dismissed him, treating him as if he were already in her past, and all the while she was doing it, she was being every inch a lady.

He wanted to pull her to him and kiss her until she was clinging to him, to remind her of what they'd had together—the passion and the magic. He wanted to show her that after the things they'd shared, they deserved more than this cool, remote parting.

But then what would he accomplish by doing that? The fact remained that very soon now he *would* be in her past.

She looked at his hand on the handle. "Would you mind? I'm running a little late."

"Yeah, I am too." He opened the door, but momentarily positioned his body between her and the car. "Is your headache really gone?"

"Completely."

"Good. But I've been thinking. You should make an appointment with a doctor and have a thorough checkup."

"That's an idea to consider," she said lightly, "but I'm sure I'm going to be fine."

He allowed himself the luxury of reaching out to put a knuckle beneath her chin and raise her face so that he could see deeply into her eyes. "Promise me something, Annie. Promise me you'll call me if you need me for anything, anything at all."

Only puzzlement showed in her eyes as she looked up at him. "Thank you, Wyatt. That's a very generous offer, but I honestly can't think of a single reason why I would need you." She slipped around him and slid into the car, and in seconds she'd started the car and was driving off.

Wyatt looked after her, feeling sick to his stomach. She'd just neatly and flawlessly engineered the cleanest good-bye he'd ever had with a woman. And he hated it.

"I've been delayed," Wyatt said, speaking into his cell phone, "but don't stand down. I expect to be there within thirty minutes." As his pilot replied, Wyatt heard Scott come into the room behind him. "Right," he said into the phone. "See you then."

He closed his phone and looked around. Scott stood at the stove, pouring himself a cup of coffee. His hair was wet from the shower, and he'd put on a fresh pair of jeans and another T-shirt. Wyatt levered himself up on one of the counters. "Taking into consideration the ten minutes it's going to take to drive to the airport, I've just bought myself an extra twenty minutes. Tell me everything you know about Annie."

Scott glanced over his shoulder at him. "Excuse me? Aren't you the one who just spent several days with her? The Wyatt I know and love has always had the ability to learn everything of interest about a woman in two minutes, six seconds flat." With a grin he took his coffee cup and dropped into one of the kitchen chairs.

"This is Annie we're talking about, Scott."

"Yeah, so you indicated." He took a swallow of his coffee. "By the way, I broke your record in Cairo last year. I wish you could have been there. Man, I was like a surgeon—in and out in one minute, fifty-five seconds." He shrugged. "But then in all fairness, I have to admit there wasn't that much of interest to learn about her."

"Come on, Scott," Wyatt said impatiently. "I've only got nineteen minutes now."

His friend eyed him thoughtfully. "You know, this is very, very interesting to me. I've never known you to show such intense interest in a woman before—*especially* a woman you just informed that you probably wouldn't be back in this area anytime soon. Call me crazy, but that sounded like a pretty definite good-bye to me."

"*Scott.*"

He absently rubbed a finger alongside his nose. "Okay, okay, but I still don't understand this. Obviously you got to know Annie pretty well while you were waiting for me, right?"

"Yeah, but there's a lot more I want to know."

"Like what?"

Good damn question, he thought angrily. The frustrating truth was he couldn't seem to put any order into his feelings about her. "Like everything you know," he finally said.

Scott exhaled a long breath and fixed Wyatt with a serious look. "Okay, here's the deal, Wyatt. I've known you a lot longer than I've known Annie. You're one of the best friends I've ever had, but I want you to understand that Annie's also my friend. Start asking questions, but if I have a problem with any of them for any reason, you won't get the answer."

It was no more than he would expect from Scott. "Fair enough. First question—has she ever been seriously involved with anyone?"

"Not since I've known her. There are quite a few young, single people in this area—crafts people, artists—and they hang out a lot together, but it's usually in groups and always very open and friendly." He shrugged. "I've never seen her seriously interested in anyone."

"Does that include you?"

With a grin, Scott leaned back in his chair and propped his bare feet up on the kitchen table. "You know, I don't think I've ever heard that particular tone in your voice."

"What tone?"

"Jealousy."

"You need to get your hearing tested, Scott. Now what about my question?"

"Which one was that?"

If it had been anyone else but Scott giving him such a hard time, he would have flown across the table at him by now and half killed him. But it *was* Scott, and Wyatt loved him like a brother. And besides, as good as he was—and he was very good—he knew Scott was better and would take him down before he even had a chance to get his hands on him. So he simply looked at his watch. "Seventeen minutes."

With the grin still plastered on his face, Scott chuckled. "Annie and me serious? Let's just say that when she first moved into the area, I was *extremely* interested, but I'm sad to say she wasn't." He grinned. "Personally, I've never been able to understand why not. You know how irresistible I am to women."

Despite the knots that had been forming in his stomach, Wyatt had to grin. "Yeah, I know." He thought for a minute. "So what about Dennis?"

"Dennis?" Scott's brow puckered in question. "Oh, you mean Dennis Patterson, the schoolteacher? Hah! He *wishes*, along with half the eligible men in the county, I might add. But I have to say, Dennis had an interesting approach. At first, he went after her hard and got nowhere fast. But to give him his due, he didn't give up. Then, he insinuated himself into her group and hung out with all her friends until Annie got comfortable with him. Then he asked her out again. By that time I think she felt sorry for him, so she went out with **him a couple of times. Inevitably, though, he got too** serious and she backed away. She told me she had to be firm about it, too, for him to finally get the message."

Wyatt picked up a fork and absently tapped it on top of the counter beside him. "I saw him looking at her, and he's still got a thing for her."

Scott shrugged. "So what? As a matter of fact, what's he got to do with anything?"

"Nothing, I guess. I was just trying to get a sense of the men who have been in her life."

Scott downed another gulp of his coffee. "Look, before she settled here, I'm sure there was a guy or two. She's even mentioned a couple of names. But I've known her ever since she moved here eight years ago, and I've never seen her serious with anyone. She's said she doesn't even want to marry."

"Yeah, she told me that too." Wyatt shifted on the counter and clasped his hands together. "Do you know why she feels that way?"

Scott's expression turned wry. "If you mean, did some man long ago break her heart to such an extent that she's decided to seal her heart against any more hurt, the answer is an emphatic no. I honestly believe it's simply that somewhere along the line she decided she liked her life just as it is. And why not? She's got all the friends anyone would ever need, she likes her own company, I've never known her to be bored, she's successful and very happy." Scott broke off to stare at Wyatt for a moment. "And actually, now that I think about it, if you were able to get close to her during the short amount of time you two spent together, then I'd say you accomplished a pretty big miracle, although . . ." He grinned. "Although she didn't seem too sad to see you go."

"No, she didn't, so you can scratch your miracle." Exhaling a long breath, he glanced at his watch. "Twelve minutes."

Watching him, Scott gave a sudden grin. "You know what? I don't think so."

"You don't think what?"

"I don't think I should scratch that miracle, because I think one definitely did happen here. *Wyatt*, you numskull, don't you see what's happened? For the first time in your life, you've gone and fallen good and hard for a woman. That alone is earthshaking news. But the fact that she doesn't seem to return your feelings probably shoots our miracle straight into whatever category comes after miracle. I've never known a woman not to fall for you if you went after her. In fact, may I borrow your phone? I should probably alert the media."

Wyatt frowned at him. "You couldn't be more wrong."

Scott nodded. "Sure, sure. Whatever you say."

Wyatt thought for a moment, then shrugged. "It's just that she's probably the most unique woman I've ever met."

Scott's mirth abruptly fled. "Yeah, I know exactly what you mean," he said, completely serious now. "I admire her more than I can say. In spite of everything, she managed to turn out to be as beautiful on the inside as she is on the outside."

Wyatt went still. "What do you mean 'in spite of everything'?"

"Ah . . . she didn't tell you." Scott nodded to himself. "I'm not surprised really. Heaven knows she doesn't like to talk about it."

"So then *you* tell me."

Scott turned his suddenly icy gaze on him. "We've just wandered into dicey territory, Wyatt. *I* know her story, because over the years Annie has learned she can trust me. But I have no way of knowing whether she would mind me telling you."

"Annie may not know that she can trust me, but *you* know she can."

"Yeah, I do." After draining the last of his coffee, Scott stared thoughtfully into his empty cup. "Annie never indicated that I should keep it confidential. Also, it's a matter of public record, and knowing you, you could find the information in a nanosecond on that laptop of yours."

Wyatt felt himself go cold. Whatever this was, it was big. Otherwise Scott wouldn't be taking the time to sort through his thoughts as he was. As for himself, he honestly didn't know why it was so important to him to know whatever it was, except it might just give him a clue that would help him have a better understanding of Annie.

Scott swung his feet off the table and sat forward. "It happened sixteen years ago. A small-town policeman in Nevada accidentally stumbled into a situation that made him a prime candidate to go undercover in the Molinari crime family. It was dangerous, but he went ahead with it and managed to gather quite an extraordinary amount of information against the organization, enough to have the headman, Roberto Molinari, and quite a few of his high lieutenants, arrested and indicted for trial. Unfortunately the policeman's identity slipped out before the trial, and contracts were put out against him and his family. Attempts were made, but the Feds did an excellent job of protecting them. When the time for the trial came, he was able to go on the witness stand and tell everything he knew. He put away the headman, plus most of the superstructure of the organization."

Wyatt had been listening intently and now he nodded. "I remember that case. It was given a lot of publicity at the time."

"It was one of those cases where the media went into overdrive, and the policeman received much more than his fifteen minutes of fame. His name was William Logan."

"Annie's father." Wyatt's eyes closed, then sprang open again. "Oh, God, Logan was killed soon after the trial, wasn't he?"

Grimly, Scott nodded. "In the driveway of his home. Thankfully Mrs. Logan had taken her thirteen-year-old daughter to visit an aunt that afternoon and they weren't home." He paused. "He was given a hero's burial, and there were a lot of medals and awards presented to him posthumously, though as you might imagine, none of it gave any comfort to his widow and his daughter. And if their grief wasn't enough for them to deal with, the organization let it be known that the contracts they'd put out on Annie and her mother were still extremely viable."

"But *why*? They'd already killed the person who'd done the damage."

"Because as immoral and corrupt as those people are, they consider their word their honor. Before Logan testified, they'd vowed they would kill him, his wife, and his daughter. They killed Logan, but his wife and daughter were still alive. To their way of thinking, it would bring disgrace to them and dishonor to their name if they didn't go ahead and fulfill those last two contracts."

"My God." Wyatt wiped a hand over his brow.

"Yeah. And can you imagine how tough it was on Annie and her mom that first year? They were given the option to go into the Federal Witness Protection Program, but Annie's mother turned it down. She said she didn't want her daughter to have to give up her identity and everything she knew, along with her connections to her father's family."

Wyatt slid off the counter and began to pace. "Admirable, I suppose, but not exactly wise."

"Annie had just lost her father. Her mother didn't want her to lose everything else too. I imagine she was right. That would have been an awful lot for a kid to bear. And the police did their best to protect them. Cops from other counties and even other states gave up their free time so that they would be guarded. But nothing happened for over a year, and Annie's mother decided being constantly under guard and living in the same house where Annie's father was murdered in the driveway wasn't good for her either. So she took her and moved to another town, near Chicago."

Wyatt came to an abrupt stop. "Didn't she realize the danger she was putting herself and Annie in when she moved them away from their guards?"

"I'm sure she did," Scott said quietly. "From what I've heard of her, Annie's mother sounds like a very wise woman. The local police kept an eye out for the two of them, but there was no round-the-clock surveillance like there'd been in Nevada. It allowed them to live a normal life, which was exactly what they needed. And it turned out well. Annie finished her education there, and her mother fell in love, and married a very nice man named Robert Whitman."

Wyatt nodded approvingly. "Smart. That way they both got new last names." He frowned. "Except . . ."

"Right. Except Annie wanted to keep her father's last name. She also decided that after spending the last eighteen years in school and part of that time under guard, she wanted to travel. Since they hadn't had so much as a break-in at their house, Annie's mom gave her approval and Annie took off."

"Alone and unprotected, right?"

"Yep, and according to her, she had a great time."

"Naturally she did." His face set in anger, Wyatt started to pace again. "With half the most dangerous criminals in America out looking for her, she had *fun*. She always has fun."

"Uh-huh. Well, eventually she made her way up to this area and happily for all of us who live here, it was love at first sight for her. She moved here, and with a trust from her father, she started her own business. If any story like this one can be said to have a happy ending, Annie and her mother's story has."

Wyatt turned to him. "How can you say that? There's still a contract out on them."

"I doubt it. It's been sixteen years now, and there hasn't been one single incident. After all this time, I don't think it would be cost effective in any way for the organization to carry out those contracts. But the most convincing evidence that she's safe is that she's alive, well, and happy."

Wyatt sank into a chair across from Scott. "I knew from the first that she was unique, but I had no idea *how* unique."

Scott leaned across the table and looked at Wyatt's watch. "You're now fifteen minutes late with *no* time to get to the airport."

"*Damn.*" He'd forgotten all about the waiting plane.

Scott rose from the table, grabbed up his keys. "Relax. I know a shortcut that can get us to the airport in five minutes. Besides, the pilot works for you, remember?"

SEVEN

Annie sat huddled in the corner of her bathtub, her legs drawn up to her chest, her arms wrapped tightly around her knees. The shower rained warm water down over her, soaking her hair until it was plastered against her scalp, drenching her body until her skin had wrinkled, and running down her face until the water had become indistinguishable from her tears.

Try as she might, she couldn't stop crying. No matter what she did, the tears kept flowing and the sobs continued racking her body.

She was crying because of the dead bird she'd found in her bed last night. She was crying because of all the spooky pranks that had occurred before that. She was crying because of the laughter, the kisses, and the love-making she'd shared with Wyatt. She was crying because of the tremendously painful headache she'd had last night. She was crying because Wyatt was gone.

In this last week, she'd been bombarded with too

many emotions. But she'd honestly thought she was handling it all until her body had betrayed her last night with the stress headache.

She'd also thought she was handling the fact that Wyatt was leaving. She'd thought so when she'd said good-bye to him. She'd thought so all the way home and all during the time she was remaking the bed. She'd thought so right up until the time she'd climbed into the shower and begun to cry. And now she couldn't stop.

This wasn't like her, not at all. Angrily she grabbed a washcloth and blew her nose. In her relatively short lifetime, she'd been exposed to more of life and its emotions, both dark and light, than most people who lived to be a hundred. She'd always been able to handle things. Why should now be any different?

Wyatt. Wyatt had been the one different element in her life this week.

But he shouldn't have made that big a difference in her life. From the first moment when she'd felt the heat from his kisses and seen the danger and passion that had glinted in his dark eyes, she'd known him for who he was. A man with immeasurable personal charm and power, and yes, magic, too, who had the knowledge and the ability to use all three to get what he wanted.

She'd also known one other thing about Wyatt Damaron. Sooner or later he would disappear as quickly as he had appeared. She'd enjoyed every moment she'd spent with him, and even now she didn't regret one thing they'd done together. So then why was she sitting in her bathtub, crying her eyes out?

Was it possible she'd fallen in love with him? No, she reminded herself. She didn't fall in love.

But from the moment she'd looked out the window and seen Scott talking with Wyatt in front of the house, a cold feeling had come over her, almost like a premonition that things were about to change. She should have been prepared but Scott's casually given news about Wyatt's departure had been like a blow to her body. She considered it nothing short of a miracle that she'd been able to keep herself together in front of them, when she'd felt as if she was falling apart on the inside.

With her tears finally subsiding, she reached for another washcloth, rinsed it with warm water, and held it over her face for a few minutes. After drying herself with a towel, she ran a comb through her wet hair and ventured a look in the mirror.

Great. Her eyes were puffy and her face was so red and swollen, she looked as if she'd broken out in some rare and dreaded disease.

She dressed in a soft T-shirt and a pair of even softer jeans. With a fresh washcloth in her hand, she went into the kitchen, poured cold water over it, and held it to her face until it grew warm. She repeated the procedure several times, then chanced another look in the mirror. Not great, she decided, but better.

She made herself a couple of pieces of toast, hauled a jar of strawberry jam and a pitcher of orange juice from the refrigerator, and sat down to try to relax until it was time to go to work.

She ate half a piece of toast, then tossed it down onto the plate. There was no way she was going to be able to relax, because she knew she had to do one more thing before she went to the shop. She had to call her mother.

At the start, she'd dismissed the things that had been happening in her house as harmless pranks, though admittedly she could never figure out a reason for the incidents. But as they'd continued she'd had to consider the Molinari organization, particularly after the bird.

So what if there had been no attempts against her mother and her in sixteen years? Policemen who had worked with her father occasionally touched base with her mother about the Molinari organization. It was run by someone new now and probably had a new way of going about things. She really didn't know, but she *did* know that vows like the one Roberto Molinari had made against her family were never forgotten. It didn't matter that it had been sixteen years. If something happened to the person who made the vow, then another person would take up the contract.

She didn't want to worry her mother and she hoped she wouldn't have to, but she needed to check on her and find out if she had noticed any strange incidents.

She reached for the phone and punched in the number. "Hi, Mom," she said when she heard her mother's voice. "How are you?"

"Annie! I'm *fine*, darling, just fine. How are you?"

Her mother sounded like her normally happy self, and Annie began to breathe a little easier. "I'm good."

"What a nice surprise to hear from you this morning. You and I usually talk at night."

"I know, but I had a few minutes to spare this morning, so I thought I'd give you a call and find out what's been going on with you and Robert."

"Oh, you know, it's been the same old, same old."

She'd learned over the years that the same old, same old was good. *Very* good. "I'm disappointed in you, Mom," Annie said, inserting a teasing tone into her voice for her mother's benefit. "Your life sounds downright boring."

Her mother burst out laughing. "When you get to be our age, darling, you'll learn there's nothing wrong with boring."

She'd already learned that particular little lesson, she thought ruefully. "So you really haven't done or seen anything out of the ordinary lately?"

"Out of the ordinary?" her mother repeated. "Well, yes, there was one thing."

Annie's heart froze.

"Last Sunday, Robert took me into Chicago to the Art Institute. They're having a magnificent impressionist exhibit, and I can't tell you how much I enjoyed it. It was simply breathtaking."

Closing her eyes, Annie said a silent prayer of thanks.

Her mother went on. "I tell you, I wanted to take every one of the paintings home with me."

Annie managed a chuckle. "I guess there were a lot of nice people in uniforms who wouldn't let you, huh?"

Her mother laughed. "And they were quite right too. Not one of those paintings would have looked right in my house."

"Not the right colors? Such a shame." She felt almost lighthearted now that she knew nothing had been happening at her mother's house.

"Right," her mother said dryly. "They were also much too grand. But, darling, I would love to show the exhibit to you. Any chance you might take off some time soon and come for a visit? I think the exhibit is going to be here for two more months."

"I'd love to, Mom," she said sincerely. A short trip away might be just what she needed. "Let me look at my schedule and check on who might be available to fill in for me. It may be hard, because the shop has been pretty busy lately. Plus, we'll be having our Autumn Fest in a few days."

"If you're working too hard, Annie, stop it right now. You hear me? I want you to get out more and have some fun."

Bless her mother's heart, Annie thought, feeling so much better now. Her mother couldn't know how wonderful it made her feel to hear her say such normal "Mom things." "I do get out, Mom, I really do, and I'll talk to you soon about a visit. Right now I need to open the shop. I just wanted to hear your voice, and you sound very happy."

"I am, darling, and I'd be even happier if I could talk you into a visit. You know how much I love Robert, but you're my baby, and I get hungry to see you."

"I know, Mom. I know. And I promise as soon as I get things straightened out at the shop, I'll take some time off and be on the next plane out."

"Great, then I promise not to nag you again, at least

until the next time we talk. Have a wonderful day, darling."

"You too. Mom?"

"Yes?"

"I love you."

"I love you too, darling."

Annie hung up the phone and sighed in relief. Her mother was safe and happy.

The pilot was waiting at the top of the stairs of the jet. "Good morning, Mr. Damaron."

"Good morning, Warren. Sorry, I'm running a little later than I thought I would."

"No problem, sir."

"Good. Is everything a go on your end?"

"We can take off anytime you say."

"Then let's get this bird in the air. I'm anxious to get back to New York."

"Yes, sir."

The two guards that had arrived with the plane boarded behind Wyatt and immediately disappeared behind a curtain into the middle compartment. While the pilot secured the door behind them, Wyatt strode into the main forward cabin and sank into the comfort of one of the luxurious chairs. Two thick folders sat on the ebony table in front of him, the information he'd asked Sin to have waiting for him.

The plane started down the runway, and the steward appeared at his side. "May I offer you something to drink or eat, Mr. Damaron? We have a nice selection on board today."

"Not right now, Stan. Thank you."

"Very good. Please ring when you're ready for something."

The steward disappeared behind the same curtain as the two guards had, and within seconds the plane was airborne.

Wyatt gazed at the folders for several moments, but instead of reaching for them, he leaned his head back against the plush headrest and closed his eyes.

And just as he'd known he would, he saw Annie, her eyes twinkling with laughter, her hair blowing in the breeze.

He saw her as she'd been the first night he'd met her—the mysterious Lady Anne of the Court of King Henry, bowing before him and leading him on a merry chase through the woods. He saw her as she'd been that dark night when he'd taken her up on the hill for their picnic. She'd been incredibly lovely and so delighted with his idea for their evening. And then when she'd seen the meteor shower, she'd become breathless with wonder. And he'd felt the very same way, except he'd watched her as much as he'd watched the sky.

Since he'd known her, she'd teased him, she'd enchanted him, she'd made him remember parts of himself long buried. She'd moved him in ways he couldn't begin to count. She'd even worried him half out of his mind the night before when she'd come to him in pain.

He remembered every single kiss they'd ever exchanged. And most of all, he remembered yesterday and the green meadow where they'd lain beside the laughing river and made love. It had been heat and magic and feelings stronger than he'd ever felt before.

But what fascinated him the most about her was her special gift for fun, happiness, and contentment. And since he now knew her past, he felt she was all the more remarkable. She had experienced some of the worst life had to offer and for years had lived beneath a cloud of fear. Yet somewhere along the line, she must have made a conscious decision to stop looking for the darkness in life and to start looking only for the light.

But this morning, after she'd found out he was leaving, she'd turned cold and remote and he'd been thrown completely off guard.

Dammit. Why couldn't he let it go? Why couldn't he stop thinking about her?

Scott had told him he'd fallen for Annie. At the time it had seemed absurd to him, but now . . .

Most of his life was spent moving at supersonic speeds. But for a few days he'd slowed down and spent an enchanted time with an enchanting woman. They'd shared so much with each other, but the time had been too short and had gone too fast.

For Annie, though, it had probably been just enough. Scott had filled her in on a few choice things about his good friend Wyatt, not realizing that Annie and he would ever really have the opportunity to get to know each other. He could well imagine the stories Scott had told her, using that humorous spin of his. For all Wyatt knew, the stories could have been true. The point was, Annie wouldn't have viewed Wyatt as someone who would be permanent in her life. She'd known the vacation he and Scott had planned had only been for a week.

And after all Annie had been through, she would crave permanency and safety above all else. So when the time had come for him to leave, she'd simply said good-bye.

Yet just yesterday she'd made love to him, intensely, joyously, without one single inhibition. And then this morning she'd driven away from him without a backward glance.

He opened his eyes. Something was bothering him, nagging at him. What was it? Was he simply trying to assuage the hurt he felt over the fact that she'd suddenly turned so cold and remote to him?

Oh, hell, he didn't know. He rubbed his face, then reached for the thick folders of papers.

Out the front windows of her shop, Annie could see storm clouds stacking up in the west and the wind picking up speed. She thought about bringing in her pots of flowers that lined the sidewalk, then decided the chore could wait.

She dragged one of the stools over to the counter and sat down. So far there'd been no customers in the shop, and with the ugly weather coming in, it probably wouldn't be a banner day, saleswise. She didn't mind. Normally she loved talking with the people who came into her shop, but today she didn't feel like being bright and personable to anyone.

Raindrops began splattering against the window-panes, and her gaze drifted back to the windows. On the other side of the street, she saw a figure scurrying along the sidewalk. Zelda, she realized. She must be leaving town soon since her house was for rent already. Good, Annie thought. She hated to see anyone lose a job, but she hated seeing people scammed out of their money more.

She looked at the sky. Wyatt had probably been in the air a couple of hours by now, high above any bad weather.

She hated that she hadn't been able to handle their parting any better than she had, but presenting a cool and remote front to Wyatt was far better than breaking down and crying, which was what she really felt like doing. Wyatt would have abhorred such a scene. Still, she wished she could have bid him a warm, affectionate good-bye.

Well, there was no use brooding about it now. He was on his way home and had probably already forgotten about her.

She slipped off the stool, strolled over to her mask display, and took "The Sorcerer" from the wall. She'd just walked back to the counter with it when the door opened and Deb Jenkins stood half in and half out, struggling to close her umbrella.

"I decided to close up for a while," she said over her shoulder. "I haven't had any customers all morning."

"I haven't either." Annie climbed back onto her stool and carefully placed the mask on the counter.

"Hey, shouldn't you have brought those flowers out there up on the porch? They're going to be ruined."

Annie glanced vaguely out the window to her flowers that were now getting beaten down by the wind and the rain. "I meant to, but I forgot."

Deb finally got her umbrella shut, stood it by the door, and came in. "That's a shame. They were so pretty."

"It's about time I planted some fall colors anyway."

Deb grimaced. "Yeah, and if you can manage it, you should do it before tomorrow night. I've already done mine—the chrysanthemums this year are in really gorgeous colors."

Annie touched one of the black feathers on the mask. "Tomorrow night?"

Deb's head snapped up, an incredulous expression on her face. "Hello? Our Autumn Fest? The same fest we have every year around this time? Ring a bell?"

"Oh, yeah, right." Annie gently slipped the mask beneath several layers of tissue paper. "Don't worry. I haven't forgotten it. In fact, I reminded Scott about it just this morning, but he won't be here for it."

Deb frowned. "How did you get to see Scott? I heard he flew in only a little while ago."

Annie gave an ambiguous gesture. "It was sort of a coincidence. I ran into him. Anyway, I didn't get to talk to him long." She still hadn't told Deb anything about Wyatt. Everything had happened so fast, and there hadn't been time to share girl talk as she and Deb usually did. Besides, the time she and Wyatt had shared had seemed very special and private to her, even while it was happening. Maybe one day she'd tell Deb, but not today. And not tomorrow.

"By the way, how did you hear that Scott flew in this morning?" Annie asked, to break the silence.

Deb settled herself on a stool. "Wow, you're really not with it today, are you? Does the name Eugene Estes mean anything to you?"

"Ah." She nodded. Eugene Estes was the general manager of the airport that served several towns in the area, and Deb had been dating him for a couple of months. "I guess I'm just feeling a little out of sorts today."

Deb regarded her for several moments. "You know, if I didn't know you better, I'd say you were depressed."

Depressed? Annie thought. Her spirits certainly weren't the highest they'd ever been, but she doubted she was depressed. "I had a headache last night and didn't sleep well." One truth, one lie. She'd better stop trying to explain herself, she reflected, before she gave something away that she wanted to keep to herself. "So Eugene told you Scott had flown in this morning?" she asked in an effort to divert Deb.

Her friend brightened. "Yes, but even before Scott arrived, a Damaron jet flew in, complete with its own guards."

Annie's forehead crinkled. "What do you mean? For Wyatt?"

"I don't know. Maybe the two guards were also for Wyatt, but Eugene said the two men were armed and stood guard over the plane until Wyatt boarded, then they boarded after him."

"He told me his parents died in a plane crash," Annie said slowly, trying to connect what Wyatt had told her with what Deb was saying.

Obviously excited to share what she knew, Deb shifted around on the stool, barely able to keep still. "His parents died along with the rest of their generation of Damarons in the same crash." Deb's eyes grew wide. "The worst part of it was the crash was caused by sabotage. They were murdered. And according to Eugene, that's the reason Damaron planes are always guarded while they're on the ground, security and maintenance are at the highest levels, and I also understand the family rarely flies together. When Wyatt flew in, his jet wasn't on the ground long enough for anyone at the airport to see the guards. He just got off, and it flew away again. But this time . . ."

Deb kept talking, but her words faded as Annie realized that she *had* actually heard about the Damaron plane crash and its repercussions, but it hadn't stuck in her mind because she'd been involved in living out her own life-and-death story.

"It was such a tragedy," Deb said, her words growing louder. "Wyatt and his cousins were little more than kids when it happened, but today they're one of the most powerful families in the world. They're a pretty incredible lot."

"Yes," Annie murmured, conjuring up the image of a dark-eyed magic man. "I imagine they are."

❖⸻❖

Two and a half hours later, Wyatt knew every aspect of the issues involved in the communication merger, along with the problems the opposition was having with the Damaron plan. He dropped the last piece of paper onto the table and rang for the steward.

"Stan, I'd like a good stiff scotch, followed by a couple of pots of coffee and something substantial to eat."

"I could start you off with a nice shrimp cocktail, sir, then follow that up with an excellent grilled steak, a baked potato, and a medley of vegetables picked from your aunt Abigail's gardens just yesterday."

"Perfect." He picked up the phone and punched out the number of his executive assistant.

"Parker? I need you to do some things for me." He spent the next twenty minutes explaining in detail the charts, graphs, and reports he needed. "Get as many people as you need to help you, but it must be done by my seven P.M. meeting. For the next hour and a half you can reach me on the plane. After that, Gus White will be there for you in case you have any questions. I'm about to call him now. Thanks."

He hung up and punched out the number for Gus White and explained the situation. As expected, Gus instantly grasped Wyatt's plan and assured him everything would be ready by the time he landed.

He closed his eyes and once again Annie floated into his mind. He remembered every detail about her, the way she moved, the way she laughed, the way she talked . . .

Suddenly he sat up and dialed Sin's direct number. Within moments Sin answered.

Without preamble, Wyatt began speaking. "I'm a little over an hour out of New York. If my meeting goes as I expect it to, it'll be over by eight-thirty P.M. As soon as possible after that—say nine P.M.—I need to call a family meeting. You said everyone was tied up with business. Are any of them overseas?"

"A few are, but the rest are either here or at their homes in the country. I'll start contacting everyone and send however many helicopters are needed."

"Thanks, Sin. It's important or I wouldn't ask."

"No thanks or explanations necessary. You need us, we're there for you. You know that."

For the first time in hours, Wyatt smiled. "I know." After hanging up with Sin, he put in brief calls to his housekeeper and his personal assistant.

The rain continued throughout the day. A couple of customers wandered into the shop after Deb left, but they didn't buy anything and Annie was relieved when they left.

The phone rang several times during the day, but Annie let the machine pick it up.

She wanted to be alone, and she didn't want to talk to anyone. At one point, she even got up and put out the Closed sign, then turned off most of the lights and sat in the dark, holding the mask.

At first she couldn't explain the strange mood she was in, but as the hours ticked by and she stared at the mask, she slowly figured it out.

She wanted to isolate herself with her memories of

Wyatt, surround herself with them, absorb them until she'd never forget a single one. And she was afraid that any contact with the outside world might destroy a part of those memories before she had been able to truly make them hers.

There was nothing logical about the way she was thinking, but then, she reflected, there was no rule that said she had to be. This was her way of saying good-bye to him, she realized. She hadn't been able to say good-bye to him the way she'd wanted, so she'd say good-bye to him in her own private way.

But in the end, the world refused to cooperate with her.

The sheriff showed up at around one, banging on the door, peering through the front windows. She had no choice but to let him in.

Stifling a sigh, she opened the door. "Sorry, Sheriff. I decided today was a good day to close early and catch up on my accounts."

"No problem. I won't bother you. All I need are your house keys, and I'll go over and do a little dusting."

"Oh, *right*," she said somewhat stunned, because thoughts of Wyatt had pushed everything else out of her mind. She handed over the keys, and he was back with them within an hour.

As usual when he entered her shop, he took off his hat. "It'll take a while for me to get these prints run, but I'll let you know if anything turns up."

"Thank you, Sheriff. I appreciate it."

He was about to leave when he turned back to her.

"I assume, since I haven't heard from you, that nothing else has happened?"

She shook her head. "I spent the night with a friend last night, then today I've been here."

He nodded. "Okay, but I don't want you to hesitate to call if something does happen. There's no way I'm going to tolerate this sort of thing going on in our town."

She was barely able to keep her mouth from falling open, but her astonishment must have been obvious.

"I know I haven't been all that hospitable to you and your friends up 'til now, but when first one artist showed up, then another, and then the crafts people came and you all decided to settle here, I figured you were some of those hippie, antiestablishment types that would want to live off the land without contributing anything back." He looked down at his hat. "Now I've had time to see that you all are a hardworking bunch and are making the town a better place."

She had the feeling that the sheriff, realizing that his attitude toward her lately wasn't exactly what she was used to, had spent some time rehearsing that little speech.

"Anyway, you be sure to call if you need anything."

"Thank you, Sheriff. I will."

She shut the door, heard the phone ringing again, and ignored it.

EIGHT

Damaron Tower soared high into the evening sky, looming above the streets, sidewalks, and noise of New York City. The top dozen floors were divided into spacious penthouses for the family. The next dozen or so floors directly below the living areas housed Damaron International, with the top floor of these levels housing the heartbeat of their businesses—the Damaron offices. No one but family members had offices on this floor, with a separate section for their assistants.

As Wyatt strode along the carpeted hallway each ebony door he passed held the name of one of his cousins on a shining gold plate.

Parker was waiting for him at the door of his office. "Everything's in order, sir."

Wyatt entered his office and took a quick moment to look over everything he'd asked Parker to prepare. "Excellent job. Thank you for doing this so fast."

"No problem, sir."

It was the standard answer Wyatt was accustomed to receiving from the people who worked for him, even when he knew the employee had performed something damn near impossible. But of course their ability to perform the impossible was the reason they worked for Damaron International. "I appreciate it anyway, Parker."

Parker beamed.

Wyatt glanced at his watch. "Ten minutes until the start of the meeting. Has everyone arrived?"

"Yes, sir. They're all in the downstairs conference room, along with Mr. White. Beverages and hors d'oeuvres are being served."

"Fine. Give me seven minutes and I'll be right with you." He ducked into his bathroom suite, which included a shower, a closet, and a dressing room. He quickly splashed cold water on his face, then changed from the casual clothes he'd worn on the trip into the fresh shirt, suit, and tie that had been laid out for him. Parker again. In seven minutes he walked out the door, looking every inch the potent force he was.

He and Parker took the private elevator down to the next floor and walked into the conference room. Immediately everyone turned toward him. With an all-encompassing glance around the room, he saw every expression from antipathy to curiosity.

With a smile and a pleasant nod, he gestured toward the large conference table. "Ladies and gentlemen, please make yourselves comfortable." He motioned Gus White to take a position directly to his right and nodded for Parker to start setting up the charts and graphs.

As soon as everyone was settled, Wyatt took charge of the meeting. "First, I'd like to thank each and every one of you for making yourself available for this meeting on such short notice. Believe me, I know how busy each of you are, but I also know how anxious you all are to resolve this issue. Every moment wasted is money wasted, and I know none of us wants that, nor I might add, does the public we're trying to service. So let's begin, shall we?"

Wyatt started by presenting the Damaron case concisely, comprehensively, and with an unmistakable air of authority. Using the charts, graphs, and papers Parker had distributed, Wyatt took them through their differences issue by issue.

He strode around the room, confident, cool, brilliant, and charming, and their gazes followed his every move. Without looking at one note, he spoke for close to two hours. When he finished, he asked if there were any questions. There was one, which he answered without hesitation. Then he asked if there was anyone who would like to add to what had already been said or who still had a problem. There was no one. A surreptitious glance at his watch showed him he'd managed to end the meeting right about the time he thought he would.

"Ladies and gentlemen, I'm extremely glad we could come to this agreement. I truly feel it's the best for all concerned. My assistant, Parker, will see that all pertinent information is forwarded to you in a timely fashion. And if you ever find you have questions and I'm not available, Gus White will always be available to answer them for you."

Wyatt shook hands with everyone in the room, assured them they wouldn't be disappointed in their decision to allow the Damarons to proceed as they had planned, then left, leaving Gus and Parker to visit with the group on a more personal level.

Annie glanced at her watch and saw it was almost four o'clock. She should go home. She certainly wasn't accomplishing anything in the shop.

She went into the back of the shop to turn off a few more lights when she heard another knock on the front door. She debated ignoring whoever it was, but when another knock sounded, she gave up. It was her own fault, she told herself. The next time she wanted to be alone, she needed to pick a better place than a shop that was always open six days a week. But as soon as she got rid of whoever this person was, she was definitely going home.

She made her way into the front part of the shop and stopped cold in her tracks. Dennis was at the door, and she felt a scream start to rise in her throat.

No more, she vowed. *No more.*

She jerked open the door, but stood so that she blocked him from entering the shop. "I'm closing early, Dennis, and I don't have time to talk."

"You're closing early? Why? Is something wrong?" He reached out his hand to her, but she shifted so that his hand fell back to his side. "Annie, I've been so worried about you. Last night your house was completely dark and your machine kept picking up. Today too. As soon as school ended, I rushed right over."

Her temper began to rise. "And you know my house was dark last night, because *why*, Dennis? Because you drove by every hour on the hour? And you know my machines have been picking up because *why*? You called me about fifty times both last night and today?"

"Well, like I said, I was worried about you."

"Enough is enough, Dennis."

He looked at her funnily. "What are you talking about—?"

"Do you remember me telling you I didn't want to date you anymore? And do you remember refusing to take no for an answer and not listening to me? And do you remember I finally had to go out of town to make you understand that I meant every word of it?"

"Of course, I remember."

"So why are you still in my life every time I turn around?"

"Well, because I'd still like to consider you my friend. I mean, you were the one who told me about the stuff that was happening at your house and I got worried. So as a friend—"

She held up her hand. "*Stop.* Stop it right now. I've told you I don't need your help, or new locks, or for you to keep my house and my life under surveillance. The sheriff is on the job now."

"But—"

"No buts, Dennis. Your involvement in my life has got to stop *right now*."

His expression turned sullen. "It's because of Wyatt Damaron, isn't it?"

"It's because of *me*. Dennis, don't you get it? You are *stalking* me!"

"Good grief, Annie, that's the last thing in the world I'm doing. Don't you think you're overreacting just a bit?"

She pointed a stern finger at him. "Listen to me and listen carefully. I don't want to see you again, I don't want to speak to you, I don't want you to call me. If you do, Dennis, I'm going to go to the sheriff and file a complaint, and get a restraining order against you." She paused to draw a breath. "After a few months if you've come to your senses, then maybe, just maybe, we can be casual friends. But it will never be anything more than that. Do you understand?"

"You're being clear as crystal." His usually good-looking face took on an ugly cast.

"Good-bye, Dennis."

Wyatt took the elevator back up to his office, loosening his tie as he went. He'd already put in a full day and it wasn't nearly over yet.

He collapsed into his chair and shut his eyes to take advantage of the stillness and quiet.

Five minutes later, he called information for Annie's phone numbers. With a glance at his watch, he dialed Annie's shop. He wasn't certain what he'd say to her, but he wanted to hear her voice.

The phone rang and rang and finally an answering

machine picked up—her voice, but on a machine. With a frown, he hung up and double-checked his watch. Her shop should still be open. So why didn't she answer? He quickly punched out her home number and got another machine. Had she gotten another headache? he wondered. Had something happened to her?

He drew in a deep breath. He was just being paranoid. Or at least he hoped he was.

God, he was tired. Grueling paces were the norm for him. He frequently worked twenty-four hours a day, flew across a myriad of time zones, and still kept going. But the pace and emotions of *this* day had knotted muscles all over his body.

He took three deep breaths, pushed up from his desk, and strode down the hall to the soundproof family conference room, where not even Damaron spouses were allowed. And the minute he opened the door and saw the welcoming smiles on the faces of his cousins, he immediately felt an overwhelming sense of coming home.

Each person in the room had the Damaron mark—the silver streak in their hair that proclaimed they were a Damaron by blood. But he and his cousins were irrevocably bound together by more than their blood. They'd gone through fire together and come out steel, and they understood one another as no one else did. More important to him at that moment, they'd dropped everything to be there for him.

Emotion clogged his throat, and he gave an uneven, half laugh. "God, I'm glad to see you all."

He was engulfed by a chorus of voices and laughter,

everyone trying to get to him and speak at once. He went around the room, hugging each one in turn and saying a few words. But they all knew he hadn't called the meeting to catch up on family news, and very quickly they settled into the black leather chairs around the conference table and gave him their undivided attention.

He stood at the head of the table and slipped a hand into his trouser pocket. "First, thank you all for coming tonight. I really need your help and advice." He paused, then quietly began telling them about the woman he'd met named Annie Logan.

He deliberately left out the personal details of what had happened between the two of them. Even if he'd been so inclined to include the details, there was no need. His cousins knew him well enough to know that he wouldn't be this serious and this concerned about someone who was only a casual acquaintance.

He explained all he knew about what had happened sixteen years ago, the contracts that were put out on the Logan family, the trial, her father's murder, and Annie and her mother's life ever since. He ended by telling them that as far as anyone knew, there had been no incidents against either the mother or the daughter, then added Scott's supposition that after sixteen years it wouldn't seem as if the Molinari family still planned anything against them. Wyatt shook his head. "But a couple of days ago I overheard her on the phone, mentioning that there'd been some pranks happening at her house. When I asked about it, she said it was nothing important."

"But you think it could be something serious?" Kylie asked, studying him.

"I don't know what to think about the pranks *or* the intentions of the Molinari family," Wyatt said, a muscle flickering in his jaw. "But I damn well *do* know that I hate not knowing if Annie is in danger of any kind. I want to find out the status of the contracted hits on Annie and her mother, and I want to find out as soon as possible."

"Just tell us what you want done," Lion said quietly.

"First of all, do any of us know the Molinari family or anyone close to them?"

With obvious regret, everyone shook their head or said no.

"Our operations span the world and involve a lot of people," Yasmine said, her long topaz-colored hair tied back from her face with a satin ribbon, "but we've deliberately never had anything to do with organized crime."

"It doesn't really matter," Sin said, his eyes gleaming with anticipation at the challenge in front of them. "We were able to take down one of the world's most wanted terrorists, along with one of the most guarded men in the world, who was responsible for blowing up our parents' plane. Compared to that, this should be a piece of cake."

"Sin's right," Joanna said, her cool gaze on her cousins. "We have contacts everywhere. All we need is a picture of the Molinari organizational chart as it is today. We need to know who has the real power and is making the decisions now. It's simply a matter of figuring out how to go about getting reliable information."

Jonah spoke up. "I have a contact in the Treasury Department who might be able to help us out, strictly on a deep throat basis." He checked his watch, then pushed up from the table. "I'll see if I can get hold of him now. Let's just hope he has clearance for the type of information we want."

"It's worth a try," Wyatt said as Jonah headed out of the room for his office.

"And if that doesn't work," Yasmine said, "I can hack into the Justice Department files."

Lion smiled fondly at his sister. "Prison stripes wouldn't become you."

Her eyes, which were almost the same golden color as her brother's, flashed. "There's *no* way I'd get caught."

Lion chuckled. "I know you can do it, but why don't we wait until we see if it's needed?"

Yasmine smiled thinly at her brother, then glanced at Wyatt. "If Jonah comes up short with his contact, I know I can get into the Justice Department computer bank, get the info we need, and get out before they even realize anyone has been there."

"I know, Yaz." Wyatt dropped into his chair and rubbed his forehead.

"You're worn out, Wyatt," Sin said. "If we get the information tonight, tell us how you want this handled and then go on up to your apartment and get some sleep."

Wyatt shook his head. "As we speak, there's a helicopter upstairs waiting for me with freshly packed luggage already on board, and a jet standing by at the airport. I'm flying back tonight as soon as we can come up with a plan of action." When he saw Sin open his mouth to object, he said, "I can sleep on the plane, but I need to get back tonight."

Sin didn't waste time with what he obviously knew would be useless arguing. "Okay, tell us anyway. What do you want?"

Wyatt leaned back in his chair. "A face-to-face meeting with whoever the Molinari head guy is these days, to find out once and for all the status of the contracts on the lives of Annie and her mother. I think they've lived under that particular sword of Damocles too damn long."

"We all agree on that," Kylie said softly. "But this is going to be tricky. We don't know if we can trust the Molinaris, and if we handle it wrong, Annie and her mother could end up in even more danger, simply because we've reminded the Molinaris about them."

"I've thought of that," Wyatt said, his expression grim.

"I don't think they'd risk lying to us," Sin said, "because if we found out later that they did, they have to know that we'd make them regret it. And a plus on our side will be that they won't know why we want to know."

Wyatt nodded. "That's true. And by the way, this is not going to be a favor-for-a-favor approach. The last thing we want is to be indebted to these people. All we want is one piece of information. If they consider that a favor, we will quickly change their minds. We want to keep our involvement with them to a minimum."

"But the minute they hear we want a meeting," Sin said thoughtfully, "they'll probably assume that we do want a favor—something illegal that we don't want to soil our lily-white hands with. I mean, since we've never had any dealings with them before, what other reason are they going to be able to come up with for our request for a meeting? And they'd probably kill, literally, to get us in their debt."

Lion's lips curved upward into a slight smile. "If they knew us, they'd know that if something is important enough, we use any means necessary, legal or illegal, to get what we want."

Sin nodded. "But it's good that they'll be prepared for a request for a favor, because this way we'll be able to catch them mentally off guard."

"You're right on all counts, Sin," Joanna said. "But whatever they'll be thinking when our call comes in, I guarantee they'll start salivating the moment we request a meeting. We'll have no trouble getting a meeting with them, when and where we want. No one ever turns down a face-to-face meeting with a Damaron, even if it's only out of curiosity."

"Fun, huh?" Lion asked, but his solemn expression implied the exact opposite. "The public sees us as American icons because of all we've been through and done, and the more private we try to remain, the more they want to know about us."

Annie hadn't seen him as an icon, Wyatt thought, his mind straying. She'd seen him as a man to tease, to kiss, and to make love to. "I tried both of Annie's numbers a while ago," he said quietly, "and she didn't answer."

"Besides being very concerned, you obviously feel there's an urgency about the situation," Yasmine said, "but try not to worry. You'll be back with her in a matter of hours, and she'll be fine. You'll see."

"I don't know, Yaz. I have a very uneasy feeling."

Jonah burst through the door, excitement glinting in his eyes, a piece of paper in his hand. "I got lucky and was able to track down my contact."

Wyatt straightened. "What did you get?"

Jonah dropped the paper in front of him. "It seems prison hasn't been kind to the Molinari group that was convicted sixteen years ago. All but two that were convicted have been killed in prison. The two left aren't expected to last long. Roberto Molinari is still in jail, but with little or no power left, and close to death."

"Sounds like a slow, well-planned coup by someone."

"Exactly. It seems old Roberto badly misjudged the ambition of the younger, up-and-coming generation of Molinaris. As soon as those of the older generation who were convicted were put in jail, the next generation stepped up to the plate. By then, of course, William Logan had already been killed. Now, this is where my contact had to turn to speculation. The Feds' best guess is that the new head of the family, which is Roberto's nephew, Allesandro Molinari, called off the other two hits on the Logan family."

"But there's no hard evidence to support that?" Wyatt asked.

Jonah shook his head. "Only sixteen years of no action against the two women." He paused. "Look, according to my contact, Allesandro Molinari is a real piece of work. During the last sixteen years, he hasn't missed one monthly duty visit to the prison to see his uncle. During their visits, he says yes, sir, and no, sir, and then returns home and does exactly what he wants. He's got a whole new operation going, and the Feds still can't figure out what he's doing. According to my friend, he's the Feds' worst nightmare—smooth, educated, and street-smart, and so far no one has been able to lay a finger on him. And the only other thing I learned about him is that he's single and enjoys women."

"A best guess is not good enough," Wyatt said, his expression hard. "Where is Molinari at this exact moment?"

"He has several homes, but right now he's at his place in Wyoming. And I checked—it has a landing strip that will take a jet."

Wyatt pointed to a number on the piece of paper Jonah had dropped in front of him. "Is this where I can reach him?"

"It's not his private number, but my source was pretty sure if we call that number, we'll eventually get him."

Wyatt nodded and reached for the phone. "Good. On my way back to Annie, I can stop over in Wyoming."

Before Wyatt could lift the receiver, Jonah's hand covered his. "Not you. You're too tired."

"I've operated on less sleep than this," Wyatt said impatiently. "We all have. I'm not that tired."

"For *this* you are," Jonah said, unmoved. "For this, you'd have to be vigilant and alert every moment. If one little thing got past you, the whole thing could fall apart."

"Jonah is right," Sin said. "And he hasn't even gotten to the most important reason you shouldn't be the one to go, which is that you're too involved. If you take your feelings for Annie into the meeting, you'll be defeated before you even get started, because then Molinari will have something to hold over you."

Wyatt wearily rubbed his face. "As much as I hate to admit it, you're both right."

"I'll go," Lion said.

Jonah looked at him. "How about I go with you?"

Lion nodded. "Great idea."

"I think it's a lousy idea," Kylie said, drawing everyone's attention.

Joanna looked at her sister. "Why?"

"I think I should be the one to go, and I should go alone."

Everyone started speaking at once, giving their vehement objections. Except Wyatt. He leaned back in his chair and watched Kylie remain cool and composed as her cousins and sister continued to throw their objections at her. They were only trying to protect her, he reflected. It was what they'd done all her life.

Kylie was the youngest of the cousins and looked

delicate as a flower. She'd gotten into a bit of trouble as a teenager, but as she'd grown older, she'd developed her own unique brand of Damaron steel.

He held up a hand. "Quiet everyone. Let's hear Kylie out."

Kylie nodded at him. "Think about it. Everyone here, with the exception of Wyatt, is up to their eyebrows in work, although I know each and every one of you would take off to do this and happily too. But I've got the Bookerman deal to the point that the ball is in their court, which gives me a window of forty-eight hours. The timing is perfect for me."

"That's not the problem," Jonah said.

She grinned. "Oh, I know exactly what the problem is. You all still think of me as a kid, which I'm not." More objections went airborne, but she simply spoke louder and eventually they quieted. "Now, granted, we know very little about this Allesandro Molinari, but it's not too hard to figure out that if two or more Damarons show up for the meeting, he's automatically going to go on the defensive, which we don't want."

"Good point," Sin said briskly.

"Fine," Jonah said. "So then *one* of us will go."

"And why not let it be me?" she asked.

"You know, she's right," Joanna said. "Molinari will be expecting one of you"—her gaze went around the table to each of the men—"a man with physical power with whom he can stand toe-to-toe and in that regard be your equal. But what if instead, Kylie shows up, beautiful and delicate, yet with a backbone of steel, a quick mind, and the power of the Damaron empire behind her. His balance is going to be thrown completely off. We already know he's a man who loves women. He would be forced to greet Kylie as a man would a beautiful woman, with courtesy and respect."

Jonah frowned. "I still don't like it. Kylie, I know you could handle him—that's not what I'm afraid of. But what if he decided to kidnap you and hold you for ransom?"

Sin shook his head. "No one in their right mind would want us for an enemy. I'm sure he knows what we did to Vergara and Steffan Wythe. The very last thing he would want is to give us a reason to come after him."

"It'll still be chancy," Jonah said.

"It's going to be chancy no matter who goes," Joanna said. "And don't forget she'll have bodyguards."

Kylie shook her head. "They would stay at the plane. I wouldn't want them at the meeting. Hey, *guys*"—she looked at each person at the table—"I've learned from the best. And then let's not forget the defensive training I've received from David."

Jonah groaned. "You know, Kylie's right. She *is* the best person to go."

Wyatt slowly smiled. "I agree."

Kylie looked over at him. "I won't let you down, Wyatt."

"I know you won't." He glanced at the piece of paper that Jonah had given him and reached for the phone. "But I'm going to make the call. We need to keep Kylie a surprise until he sees her."

NINE

Even though it was only a little after four by the time Annie got home, it was already dark. At one point earlier this afternoon, the storm seemed to be receding, but now she could hear the rain steadily increasing and rumbles of thunder returning.

Storms didn't normally make her nervous, but for some reason she couldn't seem to settle down. She picked up a book she'd been meaning to read, but unable to concentrate she soon put it down again. She paced, then realized what she was doing and made herself stop.

She paused by "The Sorcerer" mask she'd placed on the coffee table when she'd come home. The black opal eyes glowed in the candlelight and a streak of silver gleamed in a black feather.

On a whim she'd decided to bring it home with her tonight. She'd told herself she'd brought it home because it was silly to keep it at the shop if she had no plans to sell it. But deep down she knew she'd brought it home because she wanted it close to her. And ultimately she decided it didn't matter which reason had been behind her decision, because both were the truth.

More thunder rumbled and rolled. She wrapped her arms around herself, more on edge than she wanted to admit, but then the cheerful call of the teakettle whistle drew her back to the kitchen. She spooned several teaspoons of her herb tea into a ceramic teapot her mother had given her, poured in the water, and placed a tea cozy over it so that it could brew.

Something crashed out on the back porch, and she whirled toward the door, her heart in her throat. Was someone out there? She glanced at the phone. The sheriff had said to call if anything happened, but what if it had just been the wind, knocking something over. She hadn't heard any footsteps, but then she wasn't sure she would with the storm going on.

She eased up to the door, pulled back the curtain, and then turned on the porch light. She saw no one, only a pot of herbs that had fallen off the railing and crashed onto the porch.

Just then lightning lit up the sky, and for a second she could see her entire backyard. There was no one there either.

She closed the curtain, feeling foolish, because she had the oddest sensation someone was watching her, and when the next boom of thunder came, she nearly jumped out of her skin.

She went around the house, double-checking the locks, but she resisted pulling down the shades. She'd always enjoyed watching the electric light–show of storms from the safety of her house and just because she happened to be jumpy tonight didn't mean she was going to give in to her fears and deprive herself of one of nature's most elaborate shows.

She placed the teapot, a teacup, and a pot of honey on a tray and carried it into the living room. She'd already lit a fire and several candles, so if the electricity went off, she'd at least have warmth and light.

She poured herself a cup of tea, stirred in a small amount of honey, and curled up on the couch. Just then another bolt of lightning flashed across the sky, illuminating the room through the sheer curtains, and a boom of thunder reverberated across the heavens.

She pulled the mask onto her lap and began to study it as she drank her tea. Strange, she thought, how from the first moment she'd begun to make the mask, it had taken on a life of its own. She'd never once had to stop and think about what should go on it, or how or where a stone, or scale, or feather should be placed. It was as if an innate knowledge had guided her, and she'd known she would never be able to sell it.

She stroked the feathers that formed the headdress of the mask. Each feather was black as midnight, but within the black, there were iridescent drifts of ruby, emerald, amethyst, and sapphire.

And silver.

She lifted the mask closer to her so that she could study it in more detail, and for the first time she realized that only *one* feather held silver, just as Wyatt had only one streak of silver running through his dark hair.

She lowered the mask to her lap again, and her forehead wrinkled with puzzlement as she realized something else. The golden koi scales she'd used for the skin of the mask looked more golden bronze than the true gold they'd been when she'd first selected them. The result of the top-coat sealant she'd used, she supposed, but in the candlelight, they appeared to be the color of Wyatt's skin.

She paused to pour herself more tea, then took several sips and added more honey. Then she settled back into the corner of the couch with her feet curled up beside her and returned her attention to the mask.

Suddenly the eyes moved from side to side. She blinked and looked again. The opal eyes were still and a flat black that allowed no light in or out. She'd seen Wyatt's eyes look the very same way.

Slowly she traced her fingers over its lips that she'd formed from chips of the darkest rubies and garnets she could find, along with bits of bloodstone. It should have given the mask a sinister look, but instead the entire mask had a mysticism about it. There was nothing at all mystical about Wyatt's face, yet, she noted, his lips were shaped exactly like the lips of the mask.

Her eyes fluttered closed. With a start she opened them again. She shouldn't be tired, she had done so little today.

She picked up the cup and had another sip, but just as she was swallowing the tea, the cup slipped from her fingers and fell to the floor, breaking into two distinct pieces.

How odd, she thought, staring at the mess on the

floor. Each piece of the cup appeared bigger than she remembered the entire cup being. And the small amount of tea that had been left in the cup was spilled now and staining the rug black. The tea hadn't been black.

She'd better clean it up, she thought, managing to rise a couple of inches from the sofa before dropping back. She looked again at the broken cup on the floor and saw that it was now in four pieces instead of the two she'd seen before and that the spilled tea had turned bloodred.

Dizziness swept over her. On second thought, perhaps she should lie down, just for a minute or two. Her head dropped backward onto the arm of the sofa, she felt the mask slip from her lap, and darkness overcame her. . . .

Colors of ruby, emerald, amethyst, and sapphire appeared out of the darkness and slowly swirled around her and through her. Black feathers floated by her, so lovely. A few wafted close to her, insubstantial as air, then moved on. But each time she felt as if she'd been lovingly caressed. Others performed graceful ballet movements in the air.

A bright glow filled the room, making everything sparkle. She smiled, happy, even after the glow faded until there was only candlelight again.

But then the mask began to rise from the floor, slowly, surely, until it was in the air above her. She saw small pinpoints of light shine outward from the dark opal eyes and suddenly the feathers that had been drifting around the room came together and coalesced into the headdress of the mask.

And the Sorcerer stood before her.

He'd come to her, she thought with a dizzying wave of happiness. She raised her arms up to him, but instead of drawing closer to her, he simply held out his hand to her and she saw a ball of fire resting in his open palm. It burned with a ruby-red fire, then turned to an emerald-green glow, then finally became an opalescent pale gold.

She was mesmerized, for within the ball she saw dreams she'd always known, and dreams she'd never had, and dreams she'd never dared.

Entranced, she looked back at the Sorcerer. With a slight flick of his wrist, he set the golden ball free, and she watched with delight as it circled her in a captivating dance, swooping and whirling around her time and again, with such beauty and grace, she could barely breathe.

Then taking her completely by surprise, it dipped down and brushed against her arm, then quickly danced away again. She gasped, expecting to feel a raw burn from the fire of its touch, but instead she felt only a sweet warmth that spread from her shoulder all the way down her arm to the ends of each fingertip. She heard herself laugh, except it didn't sound like her laugh at all, but more like the sound the wind chimes at her shop made when the wind whispered through them. But her arm felt so good, she held out her other one to the golden ball, asking without words for its touch.

But just then the Sorcerer moved his hand ever so slightly, and the ball once more turned into ruby-red fire and its dance changed and became more intense. It tumbled end over end, gathering speed and size, and when the ball of fire dipped down to her, it brushed against one breast, then the next.

She gasped again, but this time at the heat and passion that swept through her as her breasts began to swell and ache with need and her nipples began to tighten. The same thing happened when the ball of fire, now with sapphire-blue flames, swept up her legs to her lower abdomen. A pool of hot desire settled between her legs, and her hips began to writhe. She looked up at the Sorcerer and realized he was directing the ball of fire with the movements of his hand. Before her eyes, the Sorcerer turned gold, then silver, and the air filled with jewel tones and heat.

She floated in the luminous sensations of ecstasy. The flames blinded her, stroked her, gripped her, and lifted her higher than she'd ever been before. She could see the Sorcerer, standing above her, doing nothing but holding out his hand toward her, but she could feel his touch on her skin, feel his mouth on her lips, feel his hard length inside her. The incandescent pleasures turned sparkling bright and came scintillatingly fast and soon ran together into a giant, iridescent, shimmering wave that carried her away once more into darkness.

"Annie, Annie, wake up."

She heard Wyatt's voice calling to her from far away, but she couldn't see him. Of course not. He wasn't here, she reminded herself. He'd flown off to New York.

"Annie? Wake up, honey. Wake up."

But it *was* his voice. "Wyatt?" she tried to say, but heard herself moan instead.

He slipped one arm beneath her back and lifted her upper body against him. "Come on, honey. That's it, try again. Talk to me. I need to know what's happened to you."

He sounded so worried, she wanted to reassure him, but though she tried to open her eyes, she couldn't quite seem to do it.

He brushed the hair off her face, and his touch felt so good, so familiar. She attempted his name again, and this time succeeded. "Wyatt?"

"Yes, honey, I'm here."

How strange that he was here, she thought. And how strange that he'd called her honey. She didn't think he'd ever done that before. He laid her back down on the couch, and she felt him lift away. Ah, he was leaving again. It was just as well. She was tired. . . .

A warm washcloth lightly stroked over her face, and she woke up again. "My God," she heard Wyatt say, "what's *wrong* with you?"

"Nothing," she mumbled. She tried to push away the washcloth, but couldn't, but she did succeed in opening her eyes. As if through a mist she saw Wyatt's worried face looking down at her. "You *are* here," she mumbled, her eyes drifting closed again.

"Yes, I'm here." He lightly shook her. "Don't go back to sleep, honey. Stay awake and tell me what happened. Did you take something? Has someone been here and given you something? A shot? A pill?"

She'd had a dream, she remembered. A fantastic dream. Had it been a dream? She gazed up at him. He truly was here, very real and hovering over her. "Have you been here long?"

"I just got here." He lightly shook her again. "Annie, for God's sake tell me what's wrong."

"Nothing. I was just dreaming. And quit shaking me." She could feel herself becoming more alert, but it irritated her that her words were slurring.

"Can you sit up by yourself?"

"Of course." He obviously thought she was sick, but she wasn't. To prove it, she pushed herself upright, but she had to fight to keep her balance. She'd much rather lie down again, but didn't, because she could feel his anxious gaze on her.

"Where's your phone book?"

"Kitchen." *The mask?* Where was it? Taking care not to move too fast, she shifted so that she could look around her and then she saw it on the floor, along with a teacup. What were they doing there?

Wyatt walked briskly back into the room with a blanket in his arms. She hadn't even been aware that he'd left again.

"Come on," he said, reaching down for her and pulling her to her feet. "I just talked to the hospital, and they gave me directions."

"*Wait.*" She stiffened. "Don't step on the mask."

"What?" With a frown, he glanced down and saw it. She didn't know how he did it, but somehow without letting go of her, he retrieved the mask and placed it on the table, then wrapped the blanket around her.

Why did he put a blanket around her? she wondered.

But then he once again retrieved something from the floor. The teacup, she saw, and it wasn't broken.

"Were you drinking that tea?" He pointed to the teapot.

She stared at him, but her eyes wouldn't focus. "There's nothing wrong with me, Wyatt. I was just taking a little nap." And had an incredibly erotic dream, she remembered, beginning to feel embarrassed that he'd found her like this.

"Right." He lifted her and carried her out to a car, put her into the passenger side, and shut the door. "Stay here and I'll be right back."

It was Scott's car, she realized. How did it get here? She was more alert, but there were still some things she was having trouble working out. Plus, Wyatt had walked so fast with her that she felt as if she was spinning. She leaned back against the headrest and shut her eyes.

Wyatt returned, started the engine, and they were off. She felt cool air blowing in the window and onto her face. It must have stopped raining. That was good, but where were they going? Then she decided it didn't matter. Wyatt was beside her now, which made her feel better in some indefinable way that she'd have to examine later.

Before she knew it they had arrived at the hospital. Waving away an attendant and a wheelchair, Wyatt carried her into an examining room. It seemed awfully bright, she reflected, but before she could mention it to Wyatt, a doctor was standing before her, looking into her eyes with a light, and a nurse was taking her blood pressure and pulse rate.

The hospital had a good reputation, but it had never been known for its speed of service. Then again, she mused, they'd probably never had Wyatt Damaron walk into their hospital before. He was there by her side, watching and questioning everything that was being done or said. Half of the questions the doctor asked her, Wyatt answered. A nurse walked in to draw blood from her arm, and Wyatt scowled. "Don't hurt her."

Finally the doctor finished his exam. "Ms. Logan, we'll be running some blood tests, but even before the results come back, I'm confident in saying that you had a hallucinogenic experience this evening."

She stared at him, baffled. "A what?"

The doctor faintly smiled. "Like an acid trip."

She glanced at Wyatt and saw that he'd become quiet, but a vein throbbed in his forehead and the muscles in his neck were rigid. She returned her attention to the doctor. "But I didn't take any drugs tonight. I *never* take any drugs, except the other night when I took something for a headache."

"I believe you," the doctor said. "Mr. Damaron brought in a sample of the tea you were drinking, which most likely contains traces of the hallucinogen."

She was feeling stronger, her mind was much more alert, but things *still* weren't making sense to her. "No, you don't understand. That tea is nothing more than an herbal mixture I blend myself from several types of teas that I buy at the grocery store. It's just a mix of different flavors. And I've drunk the same mixture for years."

"Then without your knowledge, Annie," Wyatt said, his voice strained, "someone added something to your tea mixture, something that made you sick."

"Have you had any other unexplained illnesses lately?" the doctor asked.

"I'm never sick."

"You had that headache the other night," Wyatt reminded her.

Annie briefly closed her eyes. How could she have forgotten that? "That's right. And now that I think about it, I had several other smaller headaches before that and sometimes I felt dizzy."

The doctor looked at her curiously. "It sounds as if someone has been trying, little by little, to make you ill."

"Yes," Wyatt said grimly, "and each episode has been more and more serious. The next episode might very well have killed you." The color drained from Annie's face. Wyatt stepped over and took her hand, but addressed his next question to the doctor. "Do you have any idea what kind of substance could have done this and how someone would procure it?"

The doctor shook his head. "Ms. Logan has had dizziness, headaches of varying degrees of severity, and now a hallucinogenic episode. Different substances would be required to affect each symptom, which means the substances could have been layered in the tea container, and as she scooped the tea out, and got deeper and deeper into the container, she came down with a new symptom. Or it could mean someone has been breaking into her house every day or two and adding a new substance each time."

Wyatt exploded with an obscene oath.

The doctor continued calmly. "As for your second question, I can't say where these substances could be acquired until I know exactly what they are. But generally speaking, substances capable of producing such symptoms are easy to come by around here."

"What do you mean?"

He waved his hand in the general direction of the outdoors. "The woods are full of herbs that would do the very same thing that's been done to Ms. Logan—that and more. There are herbs out there that will kill you."

Herbs. Something clicked in Annie's brain. "Oh, my God," she whispered.

"What?" Wyatt immediately asked. "Are you in pain? Do you need something?"

"I'd like to go home now."

The doctor shook his head. "I'd like to keep you overnight for observation, Ms. Logan, just as a precaution. You've stabilized, but—"

Annie looked at Wyatt. "Take me home."

He nodded. "Doctor, I'll call or bring her back immediately if there's any change."

The doctor started to say something, but Wyatt's determined expression stopped him. "Very well. Fortunately I think the hallucinogenic episode is over and I can find no lingering effects, but you need to watch her anyway. If there's any change at all, call me."

During the drive back to her house, Annie could tell that Wyatt was filled with questions, but to his credit, he didn't ask them. He probably sensed that she wasn't ready to answer any more questions than she already had.

At her front door, he pointed to a broken pane. "Sorry about the windowpane. I could see you on the sofa, but despite my knocking, I couldn't get you up to answer the door. I'll have it replaced tomorrow."

She barely heard him. The first thing she did when she entered her house was go into the kitchen and pour herself a tall glass of ice water and gulp it down. Then she poured herself another glass and carried it into the living room, where she found Wyatt waiting for her.

Looking at him, she felt a sense of helplessness. She was incredibly happy to see him again, but she wasn't yet ready to talk to him. He was a man of action. He wanted to do something *now*. But she had to think.

Someone who knew she loved to drink tea had been slowly defiling her body by slipping different forms of contaminants and poisons into her system. And because of it, she had an overwhelming urge to try to get herself as clean as possible. It was slightly irrational, she knew, but right now she could only do what she could control.

"I'm going to take a shower," she said. "Will you still be here when I get out?"

"I'm not going anywhere," he said firmly, settling himself in one of her armchairs.

In the shower, she shampooed and conditioned her hair, then with a loofah scrub filled with soap, washed her body until finally she felt clean. She drank the second glass of ice water while she was in the shower, then when she got out and dried off, she filled up the glass again.

She didn't bother to dry her hair, but just combed it out and proceeded to cover her body with the most luxurious moisturizing cream she possessed, as if it could offer an armor of protection from the outside world. It made no sense, but then she wasn't in the mood to make sense.

She pulled on a pair of clean panties and a nightshirt that covered her to midthigh and went out to see if Wyatt had indeed stayed. He had. He was still sitting in the same chair, his elbows propped on the armrests, his fingers steepled.

She stood in the doorway of her bedroom, looking at him. It had been a very long time since she'd felt this vulnerable and confused, she realized. She understood some of why she felt that way. What she didn't know was how much of a part Wyatt played in her feelings.

His dark eyes were shuttered at the moment, yet she knew all she had to do was ask and he'd help her with anything she needed. He was motionless, yet he exuded a power and force that left no doubt he could overcome any resistance or problem.

But it was *her* problem and *she* had to fix it.

"Why did you come back?" she asked.

"Because of you," he replied huskily. "Because I couldn't stand how we parted. Because I missed you like crazy."

"I felt the same way," she said softly. Even though he still didn't move, it seemed to her as if some of his tension eased from him.

"I also came back because I was worried sick about you."

"Why?"

"Before I left, Scott told me about the Molinaris."

"Ah." She nodded.

"And later I remembered that you'd mentioned some pranks had been happening around your house."

She shook her head. "It's not the Molinaris."

"Are you sure?"

"Yes."

"You know who's responsible, don't you?"

"Yes."

"Tell me." The two words were gently spoken, but they were an order nonetheless.

She looked at him for several moments, then reached out and grasped his hand. "Not tonight."

"Annie—"

She gave a slight tug on his hand, and in an instant he was up and in front of her. "Come to bed with me," she whispered. "I need to be held."

Without another word, he followed her into the bedroom. While she pulled back the covers, he undressed. She switched out the light, and they slid into the bed from opposite sides. She turned her back to him, and he pulled her against him so that he was spooned around her.

He heard her give a little sigh, her breathing slowed, and then she was asleep. And he was left to wonder about this slender, delicate creature in his arms whom he now realized he loved with all his heart. In some part of his mind, he'd known it all along. He loved her.

But she was a woman full of secrets and a mysterious past, something he would never have guessed about her during the first days he'd known her. They'd laughed and played together. They'd even made love. But other than her offhanded remark about pranks that she'd immediately shrugged off, she'd never once given him an indication that anything strange or frightening had happened.

Gently he brushed her wet hair back from the side of her face and off the tender curve of her neck. Light from the living room slanted into the bedroom, allowing him to see her profile, so pure and lovely. If only she'd come to him, he could have had it all figured out and handled by now and she wouldn't have had to go through what she did tonight. But he was sure it hadn't even occurred to her to share with him what was happening, and the thought drove him wild. She was too independent for her own good.

Yet she trusted him. He *knew* she did. For one thing, she wouldn't have fallen into such an untroubled sleep in his arms, assured that he would hold her and keep her safe all night long.

He cradled her body closer to him. God, what was he going to do about her? So many bad things had happened to her in her life. He wanted to make sure that the rest of her life was filled with only happiness.

But how was he going to get her to accept his help?

And how could he convince her to accept his love?

And, most important, what could he do to make her love him back?

TEN

Annie awoke sometime in the middle of the night to an immediate sensation of warmth and safety.

Wyatt.

Her head was cradled in the crook of his arm, and his leanly muscled body was curled around her protectively.

Carefully, so as not to wake him, she rolled over on her back, but in the dim light, she found him awake and watching her. "Haven't you fallen asleep yet?" she whispered, unwilling to disturb the night's peace in any way.

"No," he whispered back. "I've been busy watching you."

"Why? Because the doctor told you to? It's not necessary. I'm fine."

"I was watching you because you're beautiful." He slowly grinned. "And also because it's not exactly easy for me to sleep when you're this close to me and you—

we—are wearing so little." He gave a light tug on the hem of her nightshirt, which had edged upward during her sleep to leave her midriff bare.

"Oh." She shifted and pulled down the nightshirt. "I'm sorry, I guess I wasn't thinking. I just wanted, needed—"

"I know," he murmured, "I know. I needed the same thing." He came up on one elbow and caressed her face. "Annie, I've been crazy with worry about you ever since Scott told me about the Molinaris. To make it worse, I called you here and at the shop this afternoon, but I got your damned machines."

"I'm sorry you were so worried, but I didn't feel like talking to anyone so I let the machines pick up." She rolled over to her side, bringing her body closer to his. His warm, musky scent invaded her senses. The dark, curly hairs on his broad chest beckoned. She eased her fingers through the hair that covered the wide expanse of his chest, enjoying their texture and the way they curled over her fingers.

"You didn't feel like talking to anyone? That doesn't sound like you."

A catch in his voice betrayed that her exploration was getting to him. It was getting to her too. A few minutes ago when she'd awakened she'd felt surrounded by warmth. But now she was feeling a different kind of warmth, the kind that spread through her veins, pooled in her loins, and fogged her mind.

"It doesn't matter," she said, completely absorbed now in the shape and the textures of his body. On a blanket by the river, she'd learned his body, but now she wanted to learn more.

What would it do to him and to her, for instance, if she laved her tongue around his nipple? Eager to satisfy her curiosity, she leaned forward and bent her head to blow a warm breath through his chest hairs. Then she turned her attention to his nipple and licked, again and again.

A rough sound rumbled upward from the depths of him. He took hold of her shoulder in an effort to restrain her. "This is *not* a good idea, Annie. You need your rest."

"I slept for a while, and I'll sleep more later." A light push against the arm that he was using to prop himself up and he was once again lying on his side, facing her. "But what about you?" She turned her attention to the base of his neck and took several tiny nips. "When was the last time you slept?"

A hard shudder shook his body. "What are you trying to do to me?"

"I'm trying," she said softly, "to get you to answer a question." She delicately nibbled up his neck to his ear. Occasionally she'd stop to lick at a certain place she found particularly delectable.

He exhaled a shaky breath. "I, uh . . . I caught a few hours of sleep on the plane flying back here."

With the tip of her tongue, she outlined the shape of his ear. "You can't get any rest on a plane."

He moved his head as if he were trying to evade a mosquito, but they both knew there wasn't an insect in sight. It was her tongue and warm breath murmuring in his ear that was bothering him, exciting him. She could feel the hard bulge of his sex pressing against the *V* formed by her upper thighs and the thump of his heart-beat pounding against her chest. Its almost violent rhythm exactly matched her own.

"You can rest on a plane if it's your own jet and you have a bed in it," he said tightly.

"A bed?" In her surprise, she eased back from him.

He rubbed his brow as if he was trying to think.

"I'll drive you out to the airport right now," he finally said, "take you aboard, and put you in that bed, if you promise to go back to sleep."

"I don't need to sleep." Without sitting up, she rolled her hips from one side to the other and peeled off her panties. Then with only a slight shift of position, she skimmed her nightshirt off and tossed it over the side of the bed.

He gave a harsh groan as if something had torn apart inside him. She reached over to him, hooked her fingers inside the elastic waistband of his briefs and began to pull them down. He didn't move, didn't help. The tension in his body was palpable, tension caused by his fight for control. But finally she managed to get them down over his hips and muscled buttocks until his briefs were around his knees, and she had freed his hard, throbbing sex. She reached for it, but with a barely contained violence, his hand closed over hers, stopping her.

"Annie," he said, his voice an almost-menacing growl, "you're starting something that in a few seconds you're not going to be able to stop. Are you sure you're up to this?"

She smiled. "I've been trying to tell you that it's not sleep I need. It's *you* I need."

She didn't have an opportunity to draw her next breath before his mouth found hers and he pushed his briefs the rest of the way off his body. Then he rolled over on top of her and plunged into her.

She hadn't known she was so hungry for him, she thought hazily, until she'd tasted the invasion of his tongue into her mouth and felt the hard pressure of his lips on hers. And she hadn't realized that she'd felt empty until he drove into her, filling her.

He'd held her in his arms as she'd slept, Wyatt reflected with the small part of his brain that still worked. And with each breath he'd drawn, he inhaled the scents of her—the herbal smell of her freshly washed hair, the perfumed moisturizing cream she'd put on her already silky skin. He'd breathed her in until his senses were overflowing with her. He'd held her so close, it was as if he were trying to absorb her into him. And he'd had to practically go through hell to try to keep his body in check.

But when she'd awakened and had begun to touch, nibble, and lick his skin, his control had started to slip. If she'd stopped there, he might have been able to resist, but she hadn't. The moment she'd undressed he'd known he was in real trouble. He'd been hard as a rock and hurting in every part of his body.

But the depths of his feelings for her were immeasurable, and after seeing her sick and in pain the last two nights, he had to give her every opportunity to back away.

But he should have known Annie wouldn't retreat from anything. It wasn't her way. And when she'd told him she needed him, something had exploded in his head and he hadn't been able to wait a moment longer.

Beneath him, she was wild, sweet, and pure fire. His mind had almost shut down, and any sort of lovemaking finesse was impossible. He was out of control, operating strictly on primal instinct. He wanted to brand her inside and out with his heat until she craved him as much as he craved her. He had a savage need to make her his, to make love to her so long, so often, and so thoroughly that she'd never want another man and that she'd have no choice but to love him.

She moaned, and wrapped her legs around his hips, writhing beneath him as she accepted the power and depth of his thrusts. Again, Annie didn't hold anything back. As caught up as he was in the passion that blazed between them, he couldn't help but be humbled and devastated by her honesty and trust. She was giving him everything, without hesitation or conditions. He'd never known anyone like her.

She threatened his sanity. She'd completely taken over his body. Time and again, sharp, savage pleasure coursed through him as she arched up to him and gyrated beneath him. He could feel his climax approaching, and he didn't think there was anything he could do to stop it. He tried to slow himself down, but it was impossible. She was clinging to him, every bit as hot and out of control as he, and he was on fire for her, in love with her.

"Wyatt," she cried out, clutching him, and he felt her inner muscles begin to spasm as his own climax began and a magnificent, blinding ecstasy engulfed him. His mouth crushed down on hers, and he let himself go with her.

When Annie next woke, the morning sun was streaming through the bedroom windows. She glanced at the other side of the bed. Wyatt wasn't there, but the smell of coffee and the sound of movement in the kitchen assured her that he hadn't left.

Last night's storm was over. With the sun already up, chances were good that the ground would be dry by tonight's Autumn Fest.

With a smile on her lips, she stretched like a cat. She couldn't remember ever feeling so content and satisfied. And strangely enough, the incredible lovemaking she and Wyatt had shared seemed to be only partly responsible for her feelings. She'd felt a special and sweet kind of joy during the long stretches of time when he had simply held her.

Her thoughts drifted back to her erotic dream of yesterday evening and the Sorcerer. The doctor had called it a hallucinogenic experience, but it had been like a dream to her, a dream that was so intense and vivid, it had seemed real at the time. But it had only been a dream and it was *Wyatt* who was the real thing, and so was the lovemaking they'd shared last night.

She glanced at the clock. As much as she'd love to call Wyatt back to bed with her, she had a lot of things to do today. She couldn't wait to kiss him good morning, but not until she'd brushed her teeth and taken a shower.

Fifteen minutes later, she appeared in the kitchen, her skin washed and glowing, and her hair brushed to a shine.

The simple blue-flowered cotton dress that she was wearing floated around her as she moved across the kitchen to press a kiss to Wyatt's cheek. "Good morning."

He turned off the burner and swung around to her, a smile glimmering in his eyes. "A peck on the cheek? That's all I get?"

She grinned. "Well, you did seem rather busy."

"Sorry, but I've been slaving over a hot stove for minutes and minutes and a peck on my cheek just isn't going to get it."

Chuckling, she threaded her arms around his neck. "I do most humbly beg your pardon for my mistake, but if you'll just be patient for one nanosecond I'll immediately rectify it." She stood up on her tiptoes and gave him a deep, long, heated kiss that made her go weak at the knees before it was over. When she finally pulled away, she asked, "How was that?"

"You rectify mistakes pretty well," he said huskily, "but hang around, because I'm thinking that you may need to do some more rectifying later. And by the way—good morning. You look wonderful."

"Thanks." She laughed and peered around him to

the stove. "*Pancakes.* And with strawberries! What a treat!" She held out her skirt and curtsied. "Thank you, kind Sir."

One dark brow rose. "Lady Anne, I presume?"

"I'm practicing for tonight."

"Tonight?"

"Tonight's our Autumn Fest. I told you about it. Remember? Anyway, just about everyone comes in costume. I usually have time to come up with something new between the Ren Faire and the fest, but I just haven't had time. Anyway, I may just go as Lady Anne."

"Lady Anne certainly works for me. In fact, I have a particular fondness for her." He threw her a grin, then slid a stack of perfectly browned pancakes onto two plates, garnished each with strawberries, and carried them over to the table. Next he raided the refrigerator for butter, maple syrup, and orange juice.

Watching him move around her kitchen gave her an enormous amount of pleasure, Annie reflected, and he did it very well too. "It's hard to believe a man like you can cook. I mean, whenever you get hungry, all you have to do is push a button and food appears."

He gestured at her with the maple syrup bottle. "If you're suggesting that I had Bertha whip all this up for me, you're wrong."

"Actually the thought never entered my mind. I simply assumed you'd waved your hand and conjured it all up." She smiled. "So, how did all of this come about?"

"I found a cookbook in your pantry, plus all of the

ingredients, so I just started in." He shrugged. "I'm a fast learner."

"Amazing," she said, settling herself at the table. "You're an amazing man."

His lips twisted wryly. "Maybe you should hold your compliments until you taste the pancakes." He placed his finds from the refrigerator on the table, then back at the counter, he poured them both some coffee.

"Oh, by the way, don't worry about a costume for yourself," Annie said. "I've got it all figured out."

"Excuse me?" he said, so startled, he nearly overfilled one of the cups.

She smiled again, so happy to be with him once more. "Well, if you want to spend the evening with me, you'll have to come to the Autumn Fest. And if you go to the Autumn Fest, you have to wear a costume."

He carried their cups to the table and took the chair across from her. "Well, since I do plan to spend the evening with you, I guess I'll have to wear some sort of costume, but there's one thing I want to make perfectly clear." His tone was very firm. "Like young Harley, I refuse to wear spandex and a codpiece."

Mischief glittered in her eyes as she took a bite out of a strawberry. "Relax. You don't have to worry about a thing."

"Uh-huh." His tone was dubious.

"Actually Scott has a few costumes from years past. I was thinking in particular about a black cape and domino mask he has. You'd look quite dashing in it."

"I guess that doesn't sound too bad."

"You'll see. It's going to be fun." She eyed the coffee, then dove into the pancakes with gusto.

"Annie, you don't have to worry about the coffee having any unusual ingredients in it, because I made it from an unopened can I found in your pantry."

"Thanks for the reassurance. I forgot I had that can. I try to keep some on hand for when my mother comes to visit." She gestured to the pancakes with her fork. "These are absolutely *wonderful*. If the day ever comes that you're having a little trouble making ends meet, you could get a job as a chef, no problem."

"Thanks for the suggestion," he said dryly, "but I probably won't have to get a second job anytime soon."

She waved her fork in the air. "It was just a thought."

"I appreciate your concern." He paused. "Annie, about what happened last night."

She laid her fork on the edge of her plate and took a sip of orange juice. She'd known this moment would come, and she'd been dreading it. "Okay, Wyatt, it's like this." She paused, choosing her words carefully. "Last night was wonderful, but you don't have to worry about my misinterpreting your intent."

He looked at her blankly. "What are you talking about?"

"It's just that I know that a night of lovemaking with you, no matter how extraordinary, doesn't mean a commitment of any kind." She shrugged. "You and I have fun together, and I understand that that's the extent of it. I've always understood that."

He shook his head. "Annie, you're on the wrong

track completely. My question wasn't about the time we just spent together, although we *will* get back to that soon. But I was referring to the tea you drank, its hallu-cinogenic contents, and who put them in there. Last night you told me you knew who did it. I'd like to know who it is, so that we can go straight to the sheriff. This needs to be taken care of immediately."

Annie leaned back in her chair. She'd been truly happy this morning. Wyatt had flown back to her last night, and it seemed as if he was going to stay for a little while longer. Last night, she'd also figured out who was responsible for the things that had been happening to her, and the knowledge had come as an enormous relief. Now she knew exactly what direction the danger was coming from and what she had to do about it.

But Wyatt had just cast a shadow over her happi-ness, and she wasn't yet ready for her happiness to go away.

She shook her head. "I don't want to talk about this right now." She glanced at her watch. "As a matter of fact, I should probably go on over to the shop and open it a little early. There are going to be a lot of people in town today—some will be working on the Autumn Fest and others will be driving in for it."

He reached across the table and closed his hand over hers. "Why don't you want to tell me who it is?"

She fixed him with a steady gaze. "I want to keep you apart from my problems, because I don't want them to interfere with the limited time you and I have to-gether."

Wyatt cursed beneath his breath. "But it's already

happened. First there was your headache, then last night I had to take you to the hospital."

"I know, and I'm really sorry. The last thing I want is to become a burden or a problem to you in any way, which is another reason why I want to take care of this without you."

"It would be impossible for me to ever consider you a burden or a problem, Annie. And there's not one single reason why you should have to go through this alone when you have me to help you."

Yes, he was here with her now to help her, she reflected sadly, but it wouldn't always be the case. "Maybe I don't have to, Wyatt, but I *want* to. I'm used to taking care of myself. I'm also used to doing things my way. I will handle this, and after it's all over, I'll tell you everything."

"And in the meantime, you expect me to just sit on my hands and do nothing?"

"Yes." She cautiously eyed the vein pounding in his forehead.

"For how long?"

She hesitated. "It's my hope it'll all be over by sometime tonight."

Wyatt's fist came down on the table with a bang. "You completely, absolutely frustrate me, Annie."

She slowly smiled. "You'll feel much better if you don't take my refusal of your help so personally."

Without responding, he stared at her, his demeanor unyielding, his gaze hard and penetrating.

She sighed. "You're doing it again, Wyatt—trying to analyze me and figure out why I won't accept your help.

But you know, you really *have* helped me. You found me passed out last night and got me to the hospital. You also had the forethought to bring the tea along so that it could be analyzed. When you think about it, you've helped me quite a lot."

He continued to stare at her, his jaw clenched in frustration, his eyes like black stone.

"You're not going to change my mind, Wyatt." She drummed her fingers on the kitchen table, then hummed a little tune, trying to outlast his stare. Finally she decided hell would freeze over before that might happen. "Okay, I'll tell you what. I have a gift for you that I didn't plan to give you until tonight, but I'll give it to you now if you'll promise to quit sulking."

"I'm not sulking."

She threw back her head and laughed, and watching her, Wyatt couldn't help but smile. He'd already admitted to himself that he loved her. Now he had to admit that if he was ever lucky enough to get her into his life and have her stay there forever, she was going to be able to wind him around her little finger. What's more, he had the very sure feeling he was going to love it.

"Stay right here," she said, jumping up from the table and disappearing into the living room. "Close your eyes," she yelled to him from the other room.

"Why?"

"Close your eyes."

He closed his eyes halfway, so that he saw her when she peeked around the door frame to check on him.

"Wyatt Damaron, shut your eyes this instant or you won't get your gift."

With a grin, he did as he was told. He heard her walk into the room, felt her brush against him, smelled her scent as she moved past him, heard the chair across from him as it was pulled out and she settled herself in it.

"Okay, you can open your eyes."

He opened his eyes and saw Annie, her eyes sparkling with excitement, her lovely face graced with a broad grin. If she only knew, he thought, she was a gift in and of herself. "Well?" he asked, going along with her. "You said something about a gift?"

"How can one man be so blind?" she asked in exasperation. "Look in *front* of you."

"I thought I was."

"I mean *down*. Look on the table in front of you."

He did and saw the mask she'd named "The Sorcerer." It was an extraordinary piece of art, and he'd wanted it ever since he'd first seen it, but . . . He looked back at her. "I don't understand."

"The mask is my gift to you. It's yours now."

He looked at her, puzzled. "But you said you'd never part with it."

"What's the matter with you?" she said with a mock frown. "Haven't you ever heard the saying that it's a woman's right to change her mind?"

"Yes, but—"

"Wyatt, take it. Please. I want you to have it. It's yours to take home with you when you leave here. The truth is it belongs to you far more than it belongs to me."

"That doesn't make sense."

Her expression turned wry. "You've led an unusual life if everything that's happened to you has always made sense."

He looked at her, his eyes glittering. "Thank you, Annie. This is the most extraordinary gift anyone has ever given to me."

"With all the money that surrounds you, that's hard to imagine."

He stood up, circled the table, and hauled her to her feet and into his arms. "It's true. This gift is incredibly special to me." He didn't kiss her, he simply held her as tightly as he could. The love he felt for her was all-consuming to him, and for one of the few times in his life, he was afraid. Afraid that somehow, in some way he was going to lose her.

He was accustomed to being in absolute control. *Not* being in control scared him to death. She wouldn't let him help her, even though someone was after her. And she didn't want to fall in love with him, or with anyone, because she didn't want to lose her independence.

But now that he knew about the Molinaris, he better understood her stand against love. If she allowed herself to fall in love, she would be putting that person in the same circle of danger she'd constantly lived in all these years. And knowing her as he did now, he knew she would fight against ever doing that, even if she had to fight herself.

Well, Kylie was going to be taking care of the Molinaris this morning, and soon, he hoped, Annie wouldn't have to worry about them ever again. But in the meantime, he wanted to find the person who was after her now and kill that person with his bare hands. He didn't want to take away Annie's independence, but at the same time, he never, ever wanted to let her out of his sight again. And damn it to hell, he couldn't do either of those things if he wanted to stay in her life. Still, there had to be something he could do. . . .

She pulled away and smiled up at him. "I've got to get over to the shop, but you can come over and hang out if you like."

"Thanks, I may do that a little later, but for now I'm going to stay here, wash our breakfast dishes, and wait for a phone call."

"Uh, Wyatt? Do you even *know* how to wash dishes?"

He shrugged. "How hard can it be?"

She chuckled. "I just wish I had a camera. I bet some tabloid would pay me big bucks for this picture." She started to leave, but he caught her hand, stopping her.

"Thank you again for the mask. I'll treasure it always."

"You're very, very welcome," she said with a smile, but then her smile slowly faded as she considered him thoughtfully. "May I ask you a favor in return?"

"You can ask me anything, Annie."

"Anything? No matter what I ask, you'll do it?"

He couldn't imagine what kind of favor she'd want from him, since she seemed so bent on keeping him away from her problems. On the other hand, he couldn't imagine anything she could ask of him that he couldn't or wouldn't accomplish or do. "That's right."

"This is very important to me, Wyatt, so I want you

to be very sure before you agree. I need to know that when you say yes to this favor, you'll do it no matter what it is."

He gazed at her, puzzled, but again, he couldn't imagine anything he wouldn't do for her. "I will."

"Okay, then, my favor is this: Trust me enough to let me take care of my problem without any help or interference from you."

He might have known she'd ask of him the one thing that was going to be almost impossible for him to do. But she'd very cleverly left him with no choice. He had to do as she wished. Because if he didn't, he'd lose any chance of ever gaining her love.

ELEVEN

The day passed quickly. Excitement filled the air as the citizens of the town went about setting up for the Autumn Fest. In years past, Annie had always volunteered to help. Fortunately, this year there'd been so many volunteers ready to step forward and lend a hand, she'd decided for once to sit back and do nothing but enjoy.

Wyatt showed up about an hour after she'd left him at her house and, without her asking, pitched right in to help her with the customers. Selling handcrafted items out of a small shop was something else she was positive he'd never done in his life, but not surprisingly, he did it with ease, grace, and charm, and sold three times as many things as she did. And what amazed her the most was the seriousness and the care he brought to each customer and each item, as if they were as important to him as the multimillion-dollar deals he handled every day.

He was definitely a magic man, casting spells on one

and all, she reflected. Simply watching him made her feel warm and content, and she fought against letting those feelings slip away from her too soon.

She was a realist. She knew that tonight would bring an encounter that was going to be ugly and maybe even dangerous. But right now she didn't have to let the thought and anticipation of it rob her of the happiness she felt. And she wouldn't.

About four P.M., Harley burst into the shop. "Wow, have you checked out the fest site yet? Everything's all set up, and some people have already started gathering."

"Great," Annie said. "That means we're going to have a good turnout. And thank goodness the storm happened last night instead of tonight."

"Yeah, the full moon should be great."

She looked around at him. "I've never heard you make a comment on the moon before. It must mean you're bringing someone. Who? That cute little blonde I saw you with the other day? What was her name? Mary? Kerry?"

Harley's skin colored. "Awww, Annie."

"It's okay," she said lightly. "You don't have to tell me now. I'll see for myself tonight anyway."

Across the shop, Wyatt opened the door for two elderly ladies who'd made several purchases, bent down to say something to them in a low voice, and sent them on their way, giggling like two schoolgirls.

Annie grinned at Wyatt as he crossed back to her and Harley. "There really ought to be a law against you, Wyatt Damaron."

"Why?" he asked, his tone innocent, his eyes glittering with humor. "What did I do?"

"You flirted outrageously, that's what you did."

Wyatt's dark brows rose. "Jealous?"

"Terribly," she said dryly. "Actually, you probably made their week."

Harley shifted restlessly. "Gotta go get dressed and get back out to the site. I have to make sure that no one messed up my sound system."

"Harley and a couple of his friends are in charge of the music tonight," Annie explained to Wyatt.

Harley waved as he opened the door. "See you all out there."

As soon as Harley was gone, she set off to check each room of the shop to see if there were any stray customers who hadn't been helped, then she returned to the front room. "There isn't anyone left. I think I'll go ahead and close up."

"So early? You might miss a few sales."

She grinned. "I've had such a stupendous sales day, thanks in large part to you—I think I can afford to close up a couple of hours early. Besides, you need to run out to Scott's cabin."

"Is that a fact?" he said, pulling her into his arms and dropping a kiss on her lips. "Why?"

"Because there's a long black cape hanging in the back of the closet of his spare bedroom, along with the domino that you're going to need tonight."

"Ah, okay."

She slid her arms around his neck. "Wyatt Damaron, you really are a nice man."

"Well, thank you, but what did I do to deserve the compliment?"

"Everything," she said, "simply everything." She slid out of his arms and began to bustle around, making preparations to close the shop.

He eyed her with a grin. "Well, as long as I'm clear on that. See you soon." Then with a wave he was gone.

She watched him go, taking the steps two at a time, striding along the sidewalk, then down the path to where Scott's car was parked in front of her house. When she could no longer see him, she collapsed back on a stool.

She loved him, she thought. She loved him more than she could even begin to comprehend.

She didn't know when it had happened. It could have been when he took her up on her challenge to produce magic, or the first time they'd made love in the meadow. It could have been when he flew back to her the same day he left because he was worried about her and missed her, or it could have been today when she'd seen him charm those two elderly ladies.

There were so many moments when it could have happened, but she supposed that *when* it happened didn't really matter.

She was in love with Wyatt Damaron.

Twilight was ending and night was beginning as Annie and Wyatt arrived at the festivities. Annie pulled her car to a stop and turned off the engine.

Even though Annie hadn't said a word, Wyatt had

sensed her tension. On the surface, she appeared to be without a care in the world and looking forward to a night of fun, but he had come to know her well. He could hear the strain that occasionally surfaced in her voice when she spoke. He could see the way her hands would tremble now and then as she held the steering wheel.

Somewhere, somehow tonight, she was going to confront her enemy and she'd forbidden him to do anything to help her. So far the favor she'd asked had cost him hours of mental torment. He'd thought of all the bad things that could happen to a person, and he knew only too well how quickly something that seemed under control could get out of hand. It seemed foolish beyond measure to him that he should let her face her enemy alone.

There was only one thing keeping him halfway sane. He didn't know the enemy, he didn't know the circumstances, and he didn't know the terrain. Annie did.

She was smart and levelheaded, and in her childhood alone she'd already faced down more fear and danger than most people ever had to in an entire lifetime. She'd told him she wanted to handle this without him. It was important enough to her that she'd made him promise he wouldn't interfere. There was nothing else he could do but trust her. And pray.

"You took so many turns I've lost my direction," Wyatt said, trying at least to appear casual.

She laughed. "That's why I decided to drive."

No, he thought. She'd decided to drive because her nerves wouldn't allow her to simply sit still and do nothing. That fate had befallen him, and it had been hell. There was so much nervous energy inside him, he felt he could have run all the way here and arrived with still more energy to burn.

He got out of the car, opened the door for her, and held out his hand. She took it and slid out.

"Thank you, m'lord," she said, then started off.

"Wait a minute."

"What?" She turned back to him.

"I just want to look at you for a minute."

She was dressed almost identically to the way she had been the night he'd met her, in her dress of sapphire-blue velvet, with the lace underskirt and low-cut white chemise with full sleeves. The only difference was that instead of a coronet on her head, she'd tied her hair back with ribbons.

"Have I told you that you look incredibly beautiful tonight?" he asked.

She swallowed hard, but kept a smile on her face. "Yes, you have and thank you. And you, m'lord, look very dashing and handsome."

For her benefit he gave a swirl of his long black cape. "I'll put my mask on in a minute, but first I have an act of magic to perform."

Her eyes widened with surprise, and her face lit up. "Magic?"

At that moment, she looked so adorable that he wanted to put her back in the car, take her to Scott's cabin, and make love to her until someone else had dealt with the danger that was threatening her.

Instead, with a dramatic flourish, he threw one side

of his cape over his shoulder to reveal the jeans and black cashmere sweater he wore beneath. Then with one hand, he reached up the sleeve of his sweater and began to pull out a blue silk scarf. Annie gasped as he kept pulling and the scarf kept coming. Finally he reached its end and, using both hands, he held it out in front of him. The silk shimmered in the moonlight.

"It's the most beautiful scarf I've ever seen," she said breathlessly. "And the biggest."

He swirled it in the air around her, then draped it over her shoulders like a shawl. "This is a magic scarf," he said in a deep, husky voice. "I brought it back with me from my eastern kingdom, and it will protect you from all evil."

Tears glistened in her eyes as she looked up at him. "It's a truly wondrous and magical gift," she said, barely able to speak above a whisper. "Thank you." She tied the ends in a knot beneath her breasts. "This way I'll never lose it."

She raised up on her tiptoes and pressed a warm kiss to his lips. He pulled her closer and deepened the kiss, rubbing his tongue against hers, tasting her sweetness, not realizing until he'd done it how much he'd needed this small intimacy before the night's events began.

She was the one who broke the kiss off and eased away from him. "I know I've said this before, but you really are a magic man, you know."

He shook his head. "Magic begets magic, Annie. Haven't you figured that out by now? *You're* the magic one, and because you are, I can occasionally be."

Silently, she shook her head, disagreeing, then she

took his hand in hers. "Come on. Let's go see what's going on."

The actual area of the fest was larger than Wyatt had anticipated. Lights had been strung from tree to tree, gaily decorated booths were set up around the perimeter, selling everything from jams, jellies, and pies, to handmade crafts. Costumes ranged from Alice and the White Rabbit, to Shakespeare, to Mary, dragging along a fake lamb on wheels behind her.

On a raised platform at the other end, Harley and his friends were playing records. In the center, a wooden dance floor had been laid and quite a few couples were already out there, enjoying the music.

To his right, Wyatt saw a makeshift restaurant set up with tables and chairs that Bertha was ruling over, and for now, at any rate, it seemed to be the most popular spot. Elsewhere he saw that tables and chairs had been set up for dominoes and checkers.

Annie drew Wyatt in the direction of a booth selling pies and cakes manned by a pretty redheaded woman dressed as Marie Antoinette, but without the wig. "Hey, Deb, how's it going so far?"

"Great," Deb said cheerfully, glancing past her friend to see her escort. "Well, as I live and breathe, I do believe it's Mr. Wyatt Damaron." She held out her hand to him. "Hi, I'm Deb, Annie's very good friend, but since she's felt it necessary to keep you all to herself, you and I haven't had a chance to officially meet yet."

"Officially?" Wyatt said, shaking her hand.

"At the party for the last night of the Ren Faire"—

she gave him a brilliant smile—"I came over and offered you a platter of meat and cheese, but before we had a chance to exchange more than two words, Annie shooed me away." She made a face at Annie.

Annie laughed. "I did no such thing. As I recall, Wyatt simply didn't want anything to eat."

"I remember you, Deb," Wyatt said with a smile. "It's nice to *officially* meet you."

"Likewise."

"Are you watching the booth for your mom?" Annie asked her.

"Yep. She came dressed as a peasant because she said she couldn't stand even the thought of having her head cut off."

"Maybe you and Wyatt can have a dance later when she comes back."

"Great!" Deb flashed another smile at Wyatt. "See you then."

Wyatt managed to give her a smile and a nod before Annie drew him along to other things. As they walked, he bent down to murmur in Annie's ear. "There's no need for you to try to keep me busy every minute. I've promised I won't interfere."

She shrugged. "I simply want to introduce you to a few of my friends."

Before he had a chance to retort, she pulled him over to a group of people she introduced as some of the artists whose work she sold in her shop. Each of them had donated an item for a silent auction, and each of them had, with great imagination, dressed as their object. Their next stop was Harley, who in a long-haired wig and tight leather pants, was dressed as a rock star in disguise.

"Since he's in disguise he won't tell us which one he is," said the pretty blonde who was standing beside him, dressed as a fifties bobby-soxer, and whom Harley introduced with a blush as Kerry.

"I can't wait to find out where he got those leather pants," Annie whispered to Wyatt as she drew him away. "I bet he can't even sit down."

Since they'd arrived at the fest, Annie had been acting as a hostess for him, Wyatt reflected, introducing him to everyone, making sure he understood what was going on. But he hadn't missed the fact that she rarely looked at him. Instead her gaze constantly skimmed the crowd.

Wyatt pulled her to a stop. "I've seen enough of the fest for now."

"But there's so much more to see."

"I'll take your word for it. But now I want to dance with you."

He could almost see her mind working. From the dance floor, she would be able to keep an eye on more of the area.

"Okay," she said.

Wyatt guided her onto the dance floor and took her into his arms. At that moment, the mayor interrupted the music to announce a raffle winner of a television set donated by a local businessman, so Wyatt simply continued to hold her against him, staring down at her. "I may not let you go," he said, his tone serious, his voice low and deep.

She smiled up at him. "Who says *I* won't be the one to hold on to *you*?"

"Try it," he said. "I won't protest."

The music started again, a slow, romantic ballad, and they began to dance. It didn't come as a surprise to her to learn that Wyatt was an expert dancer. She'd yet to find anything he couldn't do well. Following him was so easy, her mind was left free to concentrate on her task.

She searched the woods that started just beyond the tree lights. Her gaze also frequently met that of the sheriff, who always seemed to be in her general vicinity. The dance floor wasn't crowded, so she had good sight lines, but nevertheless, Wyatt's dance steps led them to all sections of the floor. Somehow he knew what she was doing and what she needed, yet he hadn't said a word. It made her love him all the more.

Suddenly she saw something, a figure sliding through the shadowy darkness of the woods. She stopped and drew away from Wyatt. "I think now would be a good time for you to go ask Deb for a dance."

"Annie—"

Already starting away, she paused for a split second to glance back at him. "*Now*, Wyatt. Please."

She didn't look back at him after that. She'd asked him to leave this to her, and she had to trust that he would. As quickly and unobtrusively as possible she wove her way through the crowd, slipped between two booths, and then she, too, was in the darkness of the woods.

She waited a moment for her eyes to adjust, then slowly started making her way among the trees. The light from the full moon that filtered through the branches was pale and dim, yet it was enough for her to pick out a path. Here, the ground was still wet, muffling movements, but at one point she paused, thinking that she'd heard a twig snap not too far away from her. It was hard to tell, but she turned in that direction.

She moved cautiously, staying alert and aware of her surroundings. Twice more, she thought she heard a twig snap just ahead of her. And as she went deeper and deeper into the woods and the sound of the music grew farther and farther away, she realized that the enemy she had thought she was stalking was actually *leading* her.

Then she saw her, a basket in her hand, stooped by the base of a tree, studying something.

"Hello, Zelda," Annie said.

Zelda straightened and turned to her. "Oh, good, you're here. I've been waiting for you."

She'd always thought Zelda attractive, Annie reflected, and tonight she appeared to be as well-groomed as ever, her hair in perfect order, her dress neat and clean. But there was something different about her. Her eyes were bright, *too* bright, as if she had a fever. And her face . . . She'd never before looked into the face of madness, Annie thought, but she just might be doing so now. Ice slid down her spine.

"You never planned to go to Arkansas like everyone thought, did you, Zelda?"

"No, of course not. I had to stay here because of

you." Her gaze turned calculating. "I wasn't sure you'd be smart enough to realize I was here tonight."

Annie clasped her hands together so that Zelda wouldn't see that they were shaking. "I knew if I came that you would come too. You've been sneaking around me and my house for weeks now. Why? Did you think that switching my family pictures back and forth and leaving me roses would pay me back for turning you in to the faire director?"

Zelda laughed eerily. "My little antics really screwed with your mind, didn't they? I liked that. I had fun watching you trying to figure it all out. You think you're so smart, but you're not as smart as I am and now you know it, don't you?"

"I have to hand it to you, Zelda. You had me thinking all kinds of things." Annie began to move, at first slowly pacing back and forth in a short loop, then suddenly changing directions and pacing out another loop, but she kept her gaze firmly on her foe. She was trying to divide Zelda's attention between what she was saying and what she was doing, though she wasn't sure it would work. "And that dead bird in my bed . . ." She shuddered for effect.

Zelda smiled, pleased. "That got you, didn't it? I knew it would." Her smile faded as she tried to keep up with where Annie was. "You even called in that worthless sheriff, but he couldn't figure it out either, could he?"

"Not yet, though he has dusted for fingerprints."

"He won't find anything. I used gloves."

"Clever girl."

Zelda took a couple of steps toward Annie, forcing Annie to change the direction of her loop. Zelda watched her for several moments, her expression growing more and more frustrated and angry, as she tried to make sense of what Annie was doing. "*Stay still.*"

Annie stopped.

Zelda nodded with approval. "Now, where was I? Oh, yes. I had to make you pay attention, you see. I had to make you understand that I know exactly what I'm doing with my herbs, so every few days, I mixed different herbs into that tea you always drink."

"But how did you get into my house?"

"My daddy was a locksmith. He taught me everything there is to know about locks." Suddenly her face twisted with hatred. It happened so fast that Annie took a step backward as if to ward off a blow. Zelda's eyes narrowed on Annie. "You told everyone that I was making false claims about my herbs, but I showed you, didn't I? The herbs I put in your tea did *exactly* what I wanted them to."

Annie's chest tightened with fear. She knew it was a mistake to try to reason with Zelda, but she felt she had to at least try. "Zelda, you claimed the herbs you were selling could cure everything from arthritis, to heart disease, to cancer, to baldness. You were making false claims and preying on people who were desperate to believe you."

"See, that's what you don't understand," Zelda said, raising her voice and rummaging in the basket she held. "I *can* cure those things." She withdrew some herbs she'd picked and waved them at Annie. "Herbs have powers that most people don't know about."

"You're right, Zelda. Herbs have a lot of good uses, but you've had no training, medical or otherwise. You were simply dumping herbs into a plastic bag, slapping labels on them that made outrageous claims, and selling them, and all without a license, I might add. You can't do that."

Zelda dropped the herbs and reached into her basket for a pair of long scissors that she pointed at Annie. "I don't *need* any schooling or a license. I thought I would have proven that to you by now, you stupid woman. I knew exactly what to put into your tea to make you dizzy and give you those headaches. Then when I saw you still weren't getting what I was trying to show you, I had to make the headaches more severe."

"You certainly accomplished that," Annie said, trying to divide her attention between Zelda's face and the scissors.

Zelda's lips curved into an oddly fractured smile. "It made me furious when you ran to your boyfriend and he gave you something to relieve the pain. You *deserved* that pain, Annie. I *wanted* you to have that pain."

"Believe me, I suffered a great deal," she said, unobtrusively looking around for something she could use as a weapon when the inevitable happened and Zelda came after her with those scissors. "But the next day you took a different tack, didn't you? You sent me on some sort of hallucinogenic trip."

"Yeah," Zelda said, licking her lips. "Your boyfriend left town, and you were at my mercy. I intended your

trip to be a real nightmare, but I must have done something wrong, because I could tell you were having a
good trip. And then of course, your boyfriend ruined it
by coming back and taking you to the hospital. I knew
you'd figure everything out then."

"Tell me something, Zelda. If I hadn't figured it out,
what would you have done next? Poisoned me?"

"Maybe. But, now I won't have to. I can just go
ahead and kill you in a more ordinary way." She bran-
dished the scissors at Annie and stared at her, the un-
natural brightness in her eyes even brighter now. "I've
given you every chance to acknowledge that I know
what I'm doing. You can't say that I haven't." Rage
seemed to build in her with every word she spoke. "But
you understand, don't you, that I can't have you running around telling people lies about me?" She tightened her grip on the scissors and took a step forward.

"Listen to me, Zelda. You need help, and I can—"

"Help? You think I need *help*?" Zelda hurled the
basket aside. "You're wrong! Wrong!" With the scissors
raised, Zelda launched herself toward Annie.

Annie quickly ducked and reached for the small
branch she'd spotted earlier, lying near her feet. Zelda
was almost upon her, when Annie straightened and
blocked Zelda's raised arm with the branch, but it broke
with a resounding crack. Frantically Annie searched for
another one, but Zelda had already started toward her
again, uttering obscene oaths. Out of the darkness the
sheriff appeared, grabbed Zelda's arm, and twisted it
down and behind her so that she dropped the scissors.

He glanced at Annie. "Sorry to be a little late."

Annie put her hand over her pounding heart. "I wasn't sure you were here."

"I was, but I couldn't get as close as I wanted, because I couldn't find good enough cover. I heard everything, though, and I'll take over from here." He handcuffed Zelda, who was fighting him as hard as she could and still screaming obscenities at Annie. Annie retrieved the scissors and the basket and handed them to the sheriff, but when he tried to push Zelda forward, she refused to move, so he simply used his huge size and strength to sling her over his shoulders like a bag of flour, and carry her away.

And then Annie was left alone with only the sound of her own heartbeat pounding in her ears, trying to absorb what had just happened. She stood there until her heart slowed and her pulse rate returned to normal and then she went to find Wyatt.

Annie saw Wyatt before he saw her. He was standing off to the side of one of the booths that she'd passed on her way into the woods. He'd known the exact point where she'd disappeared, and it was there that he'd chosen to wait for her to come back. He was holding the cape in the crook of his arm and the domino dangled from one hand, and from his rigid stance and dark countenance, she gathered that he wasn't a bit happy. In fact, he looked ready to kill someone. People were casting wary glances at him and giving him plenty of room, and she didn't blame them.

She came up beside him and touched his arm. His

head jerked around. "*Annie!*" Before she could say anything, he pulled her to him and squeezed her so tightly, she thought she wasn't going to be able to breathe. Finally he let her go, though only as far as the end of his arms. "What happened?" he asked, his face dark with anguish.

"It's over."

"Are you sure?"

"I'm positive."

"Tell me what happened."

She shook her head. "Later, okay? I just want to forget it for now."

Frustration at having to wait and worry and do nothing had rubbed his nerves raw. "Tell me *now*, dammit. I'm tired of hearing that you'll tell me later."

She took his hand and felt immediately better just touching him. "I know you must be, but Wyatt, you're going to want to know every detail, and right now I'm mentally exhausted." She tugged on his hand. "Come with me. There's a place I'd like for us to go."

He studied her for a moment and finally exhaled a long, pent-up breath. "Is it away from here and will we be alone?" At her nod, he felt some of his tension ease away. "Then let's go."

She led him to the parking lot and her car and drove them to the meadow by the river where they'd first made love. Annie got a blanket from the back of the car, and then hand in hand they walked toward the river.

The meadow looked enchanted by the light of the full moon. Its glow gilded the swaying grass and turned the river to molten silver.

Annie sat on the blanket, then leaned back on her heels with her gown spread around her. Wyatt dropped down in front of her and took her hand in his. "There's something I need to tell you."

"Not now," she murmured with a soft smile. "For now, I just want to listen to the river and make love with you."

"I understand, believe me I do. You've been through so much, and now that it's all over, you don't want to think for a while. But this is very important. I wanted to tell you earlier today, but you had so much on your mind with tonight, I decided it would be best not to distract you and to wait until you finished what you had to do. But now I can't wait any longer to tell you. Annie, I have another gift to give you."

"A gift?"

"A gift of peace of mind for you and for your mother. In whatever way you did it, you just got rid of the threat that's been hanging over your head for weeks now. I promised I wouldn't interfere and I didn't, but you've also been living under another, more dangerous threat for a much longer time—the Molinaris."

A look of fear crossed her face. "The Molinaris? Oh, God, Wyatt, what did you do?"

He reached out and touched the softness of her cheek. "It's okay. Just listen for a minute. When Scott told me about the Molinaris, I *had* to do something about it. I couldn't stand the idea that for sixteen years you'd been living with the fear that at any moment someone might kill you and your mother. So while I was in New York I called a family meeting. One of my cousins went to see the new head of the Molinari family this morning and discovered that he'd canceled the contract on you and your mother shortly after his uncle went to prison."

He paused. Annie was looking at him blankly, as if what he was saying wasn't getting through to her. He squeezed her hand. "Try to stay with me, honey. Molinari told my cousin that his decision was something he couldn't and wouldn't ever advertise, but at the time, he quietly went about calling in the hit men. He told my cousin that he'd had no intention of starting out as head of the family with the blood of an innocent child and a widow on his hands." He paused again and saw tears running down her face. Gently he reached forward and brushed them away. "Annie, you and your mother don't have to spend any more time looking over your shoulder. You're finally free."

She felt moisture on her cheeks, but wasn't aware that she was crying. She stared at him, trying to take in everything he'd said and understand all that it meant. But in truth, it was too much to take in all at once. The fear she'd carried with her for so long had become a part of her, and it was going to take time for her to get fully used to the fact that there was no more danger in her life.

So much had happened today. So much had happened since Wyatt had come into her life. Her emotions had been on a roller-coaster ride. But one thing remained sure for her. One thing remained true. She loved Wyatt, and right at this moment, she needed him more than she could say.

"And as long as I'm confessing, Annie, there's one last thing I need to say to you."

"If it's that you're going to be leaving again in the morning," she said tonelessly, "please wait until later to tell me."

"I have no intention of ever leaving you again," he murmured tenderly. "Where you go, I will go, and where I go, I hope you will go." He once again caressed her face. "I love you, Annie Logan."

"You love me?" she asked in wonder. He nodded, and she laughed shakily as she tried to brush her tears away. "It seems almost impossible to believe, but all of my dreams have come true, all at the same time. I love you, Wyatt. I love you with everything I have and everything that is me. I love you."

With a groan, he reached for her and pulled her down with him until they were lying side by side on the blanket.

For several moments, she simply looked at him, her face lit from within with happiness. Then she spoke. "We must be quiet," she said, "for there are those who say that on a clear night, when the moon is full, the fairies come out to dance here and magic happens."

He slowly smiled. "I would hate to disturb the fairies, but they should be warned that I plan to make love to you and I can't promise to be quiet."

Her lips curved softly upward. "I have a feeling the fairies may understand."

They began kissing and undressing each other and pouring out words to each other that came straight from their hearts . . .

And that night the fairies did come out to dance, and magic definitely did happen.

THE EDITORS' CORNER

Shake off those stuffy winter doldrums and get ready for the first scents of spring, which are sure to charm you into going outside. But don't forget to pack the new April LOVESWEPTs in your picnic basket. We have some of your favorite authors delivering terrifically unique, terrifically LOVESWEPT stories that are guaranteed to make springtime bloom in your heart. Enjoy!

Logan Blackstone plays **DARK KNIGHT** to Scottie Giardi's secret agent in Donna Kauffman's steamy new LOVESWEPT, #882. Scottie has a mission to accomplish—to keep Logan busy so that he can't interfere with a covert plan that's been in motion for months. But Logan has plans of his own. He's on the hunt for his long-lost twin brother, Lucas, who's involved in a cult. Stuck together in a cabin, the two form a tenuous relationship of passion and respect, not to mention constant bickering and bantering. Logan and Scottie are two kindred souls who are running from themselves, but will they acknowledge that it's time to stop fearing yesterday and look forward to tomorrow? Donna Kauffman answers that question in this achingly intense story of perfectly matched adversaries.

In Kathy Lynn Emerson's new LOVESWEPT, #883, Chase Forster and Leslie Baynton promise to be together **SIGHT UNSEEN.** Convinced by her sister that she's become the stereotypical old-maid librarian, complete with feline companion, Leslie knows it's time for a change in her life. So when Chase sends an E-mail asking, "Will you be my E-mail-order bride?" Leslie answers with a very uncharacteristic yes. Granted, getting married to a man she's met only by computer is a little crazy, but as soon as she hears Chase's warm voice, she knows she's made the right decision. Chase has to raise his brother's children and he thinks Leslie would make a terrific role model for the troubled teens. So a makeshift family is born. With more than a few surprises up her sleeve, Kathy explores the intricacies of a thoroughly modern marriage.

Well-received author Kristen Robinette brings us **FLIRTING WITH FIRE,** LOVESWEPT #884. Danger had Samantha Delaney on the run, and after coming to live in the small southern town of Scottsdale, Georgia, she thought for sure that she had escaped its clutches. Samantha answers Daniel Caldwell's ad for an apartment for rent and moves into the east wing of his antebellum home. Daniel, with a secret of his own locked away in the caretaker's cottage, wonders at the demons haunting his lovely tenant's eyes. Suddenly the threats are back and Samantha no longer knows who she can turn to—her devastatingly handsome landlord or her faithful and loyal assistant. Kristen Robinette weaves an intricate and suspenseful tale that is as emotionally compelling as it is exquisitely romantic.

In Jill Shalvis's **THE HARDER THEY FALL,** LOVESWEPT #885, Trisha Mallory falls out of the ceiling into Dr. Hunter Adams's arms, and thus begins a stormy relationship that makes for great laughs and huge catastrophes. Whether she's forgetting to close refrigerator doors or rearranging his car's fender, Trisha seems to wreak havoc wherever she goes. And for Hunter, a stuffy space scientist (Trisha's words, not ours), having Trisha as a neighbor is going to be the end of him. After living with incredibly flighty parents, Hunter has vowed that never again will his life be unorganized, while Trisha has vowed that the effects of her strict upbringing will not cloud her zest for life. Jill Shalvis's fast-paced romp pairs two mismatched lovers who are stunned to discover they're mad for each other.

Happy reading!

With warmest wishes,

Susann Brailey

Joy Abella

Susann Brailey
Senior Editor

Joy Abella
Administrative Editor

P.S. Look for these women's fiction titles coming in April! Dubbed by *USA Today* as "one of the hottest and most prolific romance writers today," *New York Times* bestseller Amanda Quick delivers **WITH THIS RING,** in which a villain lurks in the netherworld of London, waiting for authoress Beatrice Poole and the Earl of Monkcrest to unearth the Forbidden Rings—knowing that when they do, that day will be their last. Now available in paperback is *New York Times* bestseller Tami Hoag's **A THIN DARK LINE,** a breathtakingly sensual novel filled with heart-stopping suspense when the boundaries between the law and justice and love and murder are crossed. From nationally bestselling Teresa Medeiros comes a new romance blockbuster, **NOBODY'S DARLING.** When young Bostonian Esmerelda Fine hires her brother's accused murderer to help track her brother down, the adventure and passion have just begun. . . . Bantam newcomer Katie Rose presents **A HINT OF MISCHIEF.** Three beautiful sisters set Victorian New York society—and a sinfully attractive businessman—on its ear when they start performing séances, in this clever historical romance of nineteenth-century America. And immediately following this page, preview the Bantam women's fiction titles on sale in March!

For current information on Bantam's women's fiction, visit our Web site, *Isn't It Romantic*, at the following address: **http://www.bdd.com/romance**

Bestselling Historical Women's Fiction

⊱ AMANDA QUICK ⊰

____28354-5 SEDUCTION . . . $6.50/$8.99 Canada

____28932-2 SCANDAL . . . . $6.50/$8.99

____28594-7 SURRENDER . . . . $6.50/$8.99

____29325-7 RENDEZVOUS . . . . $6.50/$8.99

____29315-X RECKLESS . . . . $6.50/$8.99

____29316-8 RAVISHED . . . . $6.50/$8.99

____29317-6 DANGEROUS . . . . $6.50/$8.99

____56506-0 DECEPTION . . . . $6.50/$8.99

____56153-7 DESIRE . . . . $6.50/$8.99

____56940-6 MISTRESS . . . . $6.50/$8.99

____57159-1 MYSTIQUE . . . . $6.50/$7.99

____57190-7 MISCHIEF . . . . $6.50/$8.99

____57407-8 AFFAIR . . . . $6.99/$8.99

⊱ IRIS JOHANSEN ⊰

____29871-2 LAST BRIDGE HOME . . . $5.50/$7.50

____29604-3 THE GOLDEN
                   BARBARIAN . . . . $6.99/$8.99

____29244-7 REAP THE WIND . . . . . $5.99/$7.50

____29032-0 STORM WINDS . . . . $6.99/$8.99

Ask for these books at your local bookstore or use this page to order.

Please send me the books I have checked above. I am enclosing $_____ (add $2.50 to cover postage and handling). Send check or money order, no cash or C.O.D.'s, please.

Name _____

Address _____

City/State/Zip _____

Send order to: Bantam Books, Dept. FN 16, 2451 S. Wolf Rd., Des Plaines, IL 60018
Allow four to six weeks for delivery.
Prices and availability subject to change without notice.   FN 16 3/98

Bestselling Historical Women's Fiction

⚘ IRIS JOHANSEN ⚘

___28855-5 THE WIND DANCER . . . $5.99/$6.99

___29968-9 THE TIGER PRINCE . . . $6.99/$8.99

___29944-1 THE MAGNIFICENT
              ROGUE . . . . $6.99/$8.99

___29945-X BELOVED SCOUNDREL . $6.99/$8.99

___29946-8 MIDNIGHT WARRIOR . . $6.99/$8.99

___29947-6 DARK RIDER . . . . $6.99/$8.99

___56990-2 LION'S BRIDE . . . . $6.99/$8.99

___56991-0 THE UGLY DUCKLING . . . $5.99/$7.99

___57181-8 LONG AFTER MIDNIGHT . $6.99/$8.99

___10616-3 AND THEN YOU DIE . . . . $22.95/$29.95

⚘ TERESA MEDEIROS ⚘

___29407-5 HEATHER AND VELVET . $5.99/$7.50

___29409-1 ONCE AN ANGEL . . . . . . $5.99/$7.99

___29408-3 A WHISPER OF ROSES . . $5.99/$7.99

___56332-7 THIEF OF HEARTS . . . . . $5.50/$6.99

___56333-5 FAIREST OF THEM ALL . $5.99/$7.50

___56334-3 BREATH OF MAGIC . . . . $5.99/$7.99

___57623-2 SHADOWS AND LACE . . . $5.99/$7.99

___57500-7 TOUCH OF
              ENCHANTMENT. . . . . $5.99/$7.99

Ask for these books at your local bookstore or use this page to order.

Please send me the books I have checked above. I am enclosing $____ (add $2.50 to cover postage and handling). Send check or money order, no cash or C.O.D.'s, please.

Name _____

Address _____

City/State/Zip _____

Send order to: Bantam Books, Dept. FN 16, 2451 S. Wolf Rd., Des Plaines, IL 60018
Allow four to six weeks for delivery.
Prices and availability subject to change without notice.   FN 16 3/98